ALL THIS
HEAVENLY
GLORY

Also by Elizabeth Crane

When the Messenger Is Hot

ALL THIS
HEAVENLY
GLORY

STORIES

by

Elizabeth Crane

Little, Brown and Company

NEW YORK   BOSTON

Little, Brown and Company
Time Warner Book Group
1271 Avenue of the Americas, New York, NY 10020
Visit our Web site at www.twbookmark.com

First Edition: March 2005

The characters and events in this book are fictitious.
Any similarity to real persons, living or dead, is
coincidental and not intended by the author.

Grateful acknowledgment is made to the following publications, in which
some of these stories were first published: "Urchin #2," *Cutbank;*
"Perversion #1," *Eclipse;* "Perversion #2," *Sonora Review;*
"A Vast Triangulation," *Wisconsin Review;*
"Howard the Filmmaker," *Nerve.*

Library of Congress Cataloging-in-Publication Data

Crane, Elizabeth.
    All this heavenly glory : stories / by Elizabeth Crane. — 1st ed.
        p. cm.
    ISBN 0-316-00089-2
    I. Title.

PS3603.R38A78   2005
813'.6 — dc22

                                                2004005902

            10 9 8 7 6 5 4 3 2 1

Book design by Robert G. Lowe

Q-MB

Printed in the United States of America

for Ben

my favorite

Contents

Ad

SWF, ABOVE AVERAGE on a really good day, on a bad day still fairly cute but you might want to mention that her hair doesn't look too big before she has to ask, frequently compared to a certain movie star (who shall remain nameless, a) in case you don't think she resembles the star, b) in case you don't find the star especially beautiful, and also c) because every time someone says they look like someone in a personal ad it's more like those separated-at-birth things where the allegedly more attractive person suddenly looks distorted and creepy, like Winona Ryder looks eerily like Vincent Price and you can never really see her again in the same way, or if it's a guy who's comparing himself to let's say Ed Harris when in fact he looks more like Curly), is not even remotely overweight but has finally and recently and very reluctantly joined a gym due only to her doctor mentioning something about crumbling bones, stares with open-jawed fascination when the guy at the front desk says *Enjoy your workout*, thinks better of her inclination to start a long conversation with the front-desk guy about how that's really possible, feels as though no one wants to just come out and say working out is just not fun (excluding the random stand-up comic who will make ironic use of the word *work*), and so she will be the one to say that it is not only not fun but that sometimes it actually hurts, that if there's some point at which one progresses past the hurt, she hasn't reached it, although she does love to walk and would consider playing volleyball if a rare group of non-competitive volleyball players inclined toward reassuring commentary after any errors or mishaps invited her to play, enjoys tossing a Frisbee, which she's only ever done about twice but would like to do again, believes the Frisbee crowd is a much more tolerant type of crowd, albeit a generally sandal-wearing bloc (sandal-wearing being a singly character-revealing quality, far and away less tolerable than something as potentially life-removing and unpleasant to be around as let's say smoking [which more people seem to be inclined to consider giving up], insofar as the desire to display one's feet publicly is always either present or not, and on the subject it seems like Chicago as a city is much more tolerant of and replete with sandal-wearers, unlike New York, where a healthy shame for such things is more widely practiced, plus yuck, just the idea of walking around any major city with your feet exposed to the world seems like an incomprehensible risk, which, she realizes, doesn't up her odds of meeting the perfect non-sandal-wearing man, nevertheless this is probably the only thing she'd ever actively attempt to change about a person, and she can make a really good and lengthy case, and if you really love her you'll just give in to this one thing), loves to ride a bike in places without streets (e.g., Fire Island, which for most people is only a summer community but which she believes ought to serve as a model for cities nationwide), listens to NPR but doesn't suggest you quiz her on Dostoyevsky or anything, comes from a musical/academic family, has been writing since shortly after her long-term memory begins (but has only recently profited from this endeavor due to a current lull in her twenty-five-year run of self-loathing), raised in Manhattan, relocated to Chicago in favor of affordable housing with functioning/sunlight-bearing windows, work history including but not limited to opera singing, Wendy's, network news, soap-opera extra, waitressing, talent management, private tutor, personal assistant/launderer to star of a low-rated situation comedy, rubber stamp sales, preschool teaching, depressing and mind-screwingly prolonged periods of unemployment scattered in there leading as you might imagine to even longer periods of unemployment, and numerous on-set coffee-fetching-type jobs ultimately leading to filmmaking; trained in several areas, including typing, bartending, and stand-up comedy (dropping out after being informed that she was not funny), holds a bachelor's degree in Radio and TV, *you read that right* (on the four-and-a-half-year plan due to indecision/alcohol abuse), enjoys curtain sewing, quilting, flower growing, card making, knitting, journal writing (but refuses under any circumstances to succumb to the now-popular usage of *journal* as a verb, might mention that there are any number of etymological changes she's seen in her lifetime that she finds exasperating that often involve changing nouns into verbs), still loves movies but can only name a sorry few in recent years that have been at all life-changing or even afternoon-changing (which is maybe unreasonable, maybe she should try harder to believe she could ever meet an adorable tycoon in a chat room or that she might pick up someone remotely Richard Gere–looking if she endeavored into prostitution) but then again finds the lack of life-changing movies to be weirdly inspiring insofar as it has created a drive to make her own life-or-afternoon-changing movies for other people, plus also has the sense that in Chicago if you go to a movie alone and happen to run into someone, the response is likely to be a well-meaning but loneliness-implying *I'd have gone with you* as opposed to the implicit understanding of New Yorkers for the need to be separate from the presence of others (given that others are so frequently and intrusively present), leading to a solemn nod at most; unashamedly loves a broad range of chick singers (okay, some shame), excluding only country and/or any sort of post–Aretha Franklin melisma, believes in god but would have to double the length of this ad to explain what it is she does and doesn't believe, encompassing all god-related doubts, questions, and fears, after extensive research determined that it is better for everyone involved if she doesn't drink (coming to this conclusion after one of the more prolonged periods of unemployment in which beer and sofa became her primary fields of interest, coupled with a tendency to find boyfriends who seemed considerably more appealing under the influence of large quantities of beer, unable to give up beer by sheer force of will, joined a twelve-step program that not only helped her with the beer/sofa issue, subtracting beer/sofa from the equation actually helped her in bunches of ways, such as she can actually go to a party now and not be completely terrified of saying something unbelievably stupid, or being able to find meaningful work, or generally getting along in the world more comfortably without being in some state of unconsciousness, although the etymology thing resurfaces again here because there is a tendency in twelve-step programs to create words and phrases that don't exist outside of twelve-step programs, e.g., *uncomfortability* or *family of origin* or *rage* as a verb or phrases like *my last drunk* meaning not the last drunk person they dated [or possibly owned?] but to mean the last time they drank and maybe those two extra words are a time consideration? which wouldn't explain the extra four syllables in *uncomfortability* when one could simply use the less wieldy *discomfort*, except when considering that alcoholics seem to like having a word that indicates a greater discomfort than non-alcoholic discomfort), has some lingering driving issues (e.g., does not enjoy passengers/left turns/the expressway/snow/rain/dew) but drives anyway since the closest el stop is a mile away and the buses are intolerably slow (plus the space invasions are too numerous to even list, there's a lot of food on the bus, e.g., buttered corn on a stick is popular, which really you just don't want to get too close to); defects of character include but are not necessarily limited to excessive fascination with self, not to be confused with selfishness or vanity, vanity, a tendency to shout when things don't go her way (more often than not, in the privacy of her own home), e.g., printers jamming repeatedly or not being able to reach an actual operator after punching numbers into ComEd's automated voice system repeatedly or pretty much anything that happens repeatedly, unsuccessful repetition of any kind has resulted in shouting, occasionally regarded by others as delusional (at least with regard to who she thinks will date her, whether they're twenty-five or possibly a movie star), has an obsession with buying three books for every one read, a tendency to believe that large numbers of candles/office supplies/antique clocks/valentines/photos/toys will result in some sort of self-improvement, and a serious television addiction (more accurately, the television is usually on if she is in any way awake, whether or not it's being paid attention to, however there is generally and simultaneously a laptop in her lap, any one of the six books/magazines/journals she's usually reading at one time in her lap, an art/textile/bead/yarn-related project in her lap, dinner or a snack food somewhere near her lap, not nearly often enough is there anything warm and lifelike in or near her lap, could easily be persuaded to turn off the television in order to fully participate if pleasurable lap-oriented activity seemed imminent); in search of Owen Wilson for long-term relationship possibly involving children and a simple but elegant ceremony in which she gets to wear some beautiful whitish possibly vintage dress, with a gardenia in her hair, or some other little fragrant blossoms (and on which occasion she would certainly not subject her very best girlfriends to wearing something hideous in any misguided attempt to offset her own glory), in which there are maybe some little kids in velvet tossing rose petals down the aisle, in which they have a bonfire and a weenie roast on the beach and a cake made of marshmallows, in which everyone goes swimming in their fancy clothes, in which friends come from far and also from wide to celebrate their unprecedented great love, in which toasts are made in memory of her mom, in which she will probably mess up her makeup walking down the aisle wishing her mom was there, in which her stepdad will say that she is there, which she will understand but will prefer his meaning to be literal, that he would then say, *No really she's right there,* and there she would be, on the bride's side of the aisle, in a tasteful and *timeless* silk suit (she was always willing to spend money on any *timeless* garment *as an investment*) and expensive shoes (a concession to her daughter imploring her to treat herself to one really nice pair of neutral shoes instead of forty pairs of identical shoes in every color from Payless), wiping her eyes with a typically wrinkly embroidered hanky from the bottom of her purse, but also whispering to her stepfather something like *Finally!* and making a face about somebody's tacky and not-at-all-timeless outfit, is figuring that if her mom doesn't show up from the afterlife to attend her simple but elegant wedding, she can't imagine when she would come, unless she has kids right away, maybe then she would come; not in search of an Owen Wilson "type," not ISO anyone who looks, acts, sounds like, or does an impression of Owen Wilson, in search of the actual Owen Wilson; feels that the problem with these ads is that there's a valley between how people portray themselves and how they actually are, between what they are looking for and what actually responds (has one brief but compellingly unfortunate prior experience with personal ads in which one respondent who described himself as a handsome and well-dressed forty-year-old in fact could only be compared to Deputy Dog, if D. Dog had a comb-over and wore a soiled t-shirt with pleated pants and was closer to sixty and not a cartoon), that it seems like maybe people are not only not being truthful enough, they're not being specific enough and so has decided to try to set a precedent with regard to specificity, of course that said, she's unable to specify what O.W. should be like, since he's already like whatever he's like, and realizes that the phrase *seeks Owen Wilson* is an unusual phrase to stumble across while reading the personal ads except imagine you're Owen Wilson, and you're reading the personal ads, which is admittedly unlikely to begin with but imagine that someone who knows you, Owen Wilson, reads the personal ads and bothers to read this kind of long one and then passes it on to you, and it's maybe a little weird, still, you read past the first few pages and get to the part where it says *seeks Owen Wilson* and not even *seeks Owen Wilson type*, imagine that, because it seems possible that you might be flattered, maybe you'd even feel luckier than usual that you were Owen Wilson (in the same way that some larger group of guys might feel lucky that they were 25–45, attractive, and successful), especially if there were any possibility that there were other days when you might feel that there were drawbacks to being Owen Wilson, such as even having to incorporate the word *paparazzi* into your vocabulary and trying to say it with any kind of seriousness, or having to fire your former personal assistant for napping in your bed in your pj's while you were out, which was a particular bummer because you really thought of him as a bud, or like if your brother got picked to be *People's* Sexiest Man Alive but you didn't, or worse, like if they were considering having Sexiest Brothers Alive but then for some reason decided that your brother Luke by himself was the better choice, or constantly wondering if people were only interested in you because you were Owen Wilson, which it should be made clear is not what's happening here because if you were Owen Wilson but you were any kind of a tool she would be as uninterested in getting involved as she would be with any other less-famous tool; the hope is that O.W. will exhibit an inviting and exhilarating humanity but also maybe it would be good if they were sort of equal, that maybe Owen Wilson also has some tolerable habits or defects of character, almost any manner of insecurity is acceptable and almost welcome as it tends to make her feel more normal to hang around people who also let's say have occasional afternoon-ruining relapses into self-doubt or if it turns out he spends a little too much in the way of both time and products trying to get his hair to look like that, that would be all right, but maybe it should also be said that it's totally unacceptable if the insecurities make the other person feel inferior in any way (see: the whole "tool" thing); while she absolutely believes in the possibility that some non-actual Owen Wilson could amuse and entertain and hopefully arouse her interest just as much as the actual Owen Wilson, she hasn't met such a person thus far or she wouldn't be placing an ad, especially one that potentially portrays her as a stalker of any kind, which she is not, she would totally walk away from anyone Owen Wilson or non–O.W. who wasn't moved by her possibly certain-movie-star looks and slightly above-average, if cluttered, mind, that is to say she's as familiar with rejection as anyone and is generally not inclined to try to reverse any rejection-oriented decisions as she understands that to be futile (having on occasion been in the position of rejecting and grateful not to have any stalking situations inflicted upon her), in other words is willing to suffer the rejection but not willing to sit around anymore waiting for any Owen Wilsons, real or otherwise, to come knocking on her door just out of the blue or something; realizes that a story in the form of a personal ad potentially invites a variety of criticism, e.g., *thinly veiled autobiography of previous work reaches unprecedented levels of self-consciousness,* that sort of thing, also realizes that just because she realizes it doesn't mean it still won't happen, autobiography is veiled at least insofar as the author of this personal ad is actually spoken for and therefore does not wish to mislead Owen Wilson into thinking she is available while also not meaning to diminish his appeal in any way, supposes that her boyfriend who admits to a crush on Drew Barrymore wouldn't freak out if she admitted to finding Owen Wilson appealing given the likelihood of either of them meeting and subsequently dating Drew Barrymore and Owen Wilson via the personal ads, although writing this her mind is already going to the bad place wherein Owen Wilson reads the personal ad and shows it to Drew Barrymore, who somehow finds out who the author's boyfriend is and where he lives and then flies on her private jet to Chicago and they meet and she jets the author's boyfriend away and they have lobster and truffles in their water bed on the private jet and laugh about leaving the SWF behind and Owen Wilson is already in a serious relationship and not even with Salma Hayek or whoever but with like some over-hyped author she thinks is particularly bad; anyway, after that little digression the wrap-up becomes a bit problematic in that you now know that this has a happy non–Owen Wilson ending, but that seems fitting under the circumstances.

Urchin #2

CHARLOTTE ANNE BYERS, age eight, gets off the 104 at 63rd and Broadway at dusk and descends the cement stairs to the stage entrance of the New York State Theater like she knows what she's doing, which she does, but only marginally, and any appearance of deliberation is only a lucky coincidence. Charlotte Anne does know where she's going, but at this point, why is of no great concern. (Why being ostensibly due to her employment but motivated by other things entirely, some of which she's aware of and some of which it only looks like she's aware of.) Charlotte Anne Byers is in the children's chorus in New York City Opera's fall production of *La Bohème*, for which she has been required to audition in spite of the fact that her mother is featured in the role of Musetta, the saucy tart who dares to remove her shoe out of doors at a crowded café on the Left Bank of Paris. (Any speculation about her mother's typecasting can be put to rest, which is not to say that Charlotte Anne's mother is or is not saucy and/or a tart, but that unlike other theatrical fields of entertainment where one's apparent individual qualities such as saucy tartness might aid in their casting, in opera it helps to come to the table with some level of skill, and so if her mother were let's say of any formidable size, which she isn't, but for the sake of making this clear, if she were, it would not prevent her from being cast as a saucy tart if she could sing well enough, or possibly if she had modest talents, say if she had some training and maybe sang out of tune occasionally [in spite of the training] but slept with the right person, which her mother never does, sleep with people for that purpose, and which, in any case, could just as easily result in her casting in some non-tarty role even though, clearly, a tartiness would be perpetuating itself in order to obtain the possibly non-tarty role.) It happens that Charlotte Anne can also sing, and so impressed Miss Homan, the director of the children's chorus, with her rendition of "Go Tell Aunt Rhody" that she was cast as Urchin #2 and fitted for the green velvet costume, which she loved because it reminded her of Scarlett O'Hara's curtain dress. She had already seen *Gone With the Wind* three times, at the movies. If there is any suspicion of dubiousness regarding the matter of Charlotte Anne's casting, it is not recognized by anyone as nepotism, more like a sort of carnival thing where the bearded lady's kids end up in the show because they have beards too. Urchins #3, 4, and 6 are also children of those in the company, competent singers all.

A gift box of thin mints is passed around in the dressing room, let's say they're from the suitor of an attractive chorister, and tonight for some reason, Charlotte Anne, who would eat sugar with a spoon if there were nothing else, doesn't feel like eating her chocolate-covered thin mint and decides to save it for later in between the waistbands of her three petticoats. Charlotte Anne Byers, still eight, is right this minute thinking she maybe doesn't want to add the extra calories on account of Dante DiMedici, the boys' soloist, having said, "Hi, Charlie," at yesterday's rehearsal, not knowing that no one called her that ever, not having any way of knowing that she would occasionally ask to be called Charlie (like the perfume, signed with a squiggle under it) to no avail, particularly by her mother, who of course always called her Charlotte Anne (leaving her mother no recourse, in the event of misbehavior, but to add "Byers" at the end, seeing as how the already formal-sounding "Charlotte Anne" had the potential, every time, to inspire worry, in and of itself without the "Byers" at the end, although it wasn't too often that the full Charlotte Anne Byers combination was necessary, which tended to be for situations in which Charlotte Anne maybe spaced out [leaving something in something else for too long/doing some thing without doing some other thing/leaving something on/off/open/out/somewhere], or acted like an eight-year-old [touching/watching/seeing/looking at/saying/doing something she wasn't supposed to touch/watch/ see/look at/say/do], which, don't forget she is, eight), and even though she wouldn't know that Dante DiMedici, at twelve, is thinking more about a sandwich than anything else right now (and is not yet thinking even in broad terms about his preference in gender, let alone one specific person), such as expressing something above and beyond a greeting when he said the words "Hi, Charlie," and although she suspects otherwise, Dante DiMedici is probably not at all meaning to convey any type of psychic connection by way of his calling her Charlie without having been asked, and by extension, via the psychic connection, saying to Charlotte Anne/Charlie anything like "I care about you enough to psychically intuit your wish to be called Charlie and maybe you might like to go see *Love Story* with me sometime," which movie choice he would also have to have psychically intuited, seeing as how this is also a favorite of hers, even though she is, still, eight.

Eight-year-old opera-singing *Gone With the Wind/Love Story*—watching Charlotte Anne Byers may have a certain sophistication slightly above the average eight-year-old's, but that may have no bearing on whether she is going to think through what might happen to a chocolate-covered thin mint situated between the waistbands of her three petticoats, and as such, this chocolate-covered thin mint is promptly forgotten about for the duration of her appearance in the second act, largely because of Dante DiMedici being the cutest thing ever, in spite of his undetermined gender preferences, the age difference, or the difference in their heights, which is not in his favor, which lack of height Charlotte Anne's mother explains by way of saying that Dante had been castrated by his own mother (in order to preserve his glorious soprano), and even though Charlotte Anne doesn't know what castrated is, and even though she would have no reason, even if she did, to rethink her crush on the basis of this information, seeing as how (one would hope) eight-year-old Charlotte Anne would have no particular use for/cause to see/need to see such parts at this time. Charlotte Anne has only a peripheral awareness, at this time, that her mother is given to drama (and therefore lending a lack of credibility to the castration theory, which Charlotte Anne, at eight, wouldn't know was not currently in practice), and also does not know that her mother is carrying some unspecified resentment toward Dante DiMedici's mother, and thus, that the possibility is present that this accusation is of dubious origin at best. (It wouldn't be a year before her mother would just come out and say that Dante Di-Medici got his balls cut off, which, needless to say, even to *Gone With the Wind/Love Story*—watching, public-transportation-taking

Charlotte Anne, is disturbing, naturally, since this explanation comes not very long at all after she finds out what balls even are, and at eight, with only a slightly more developed awareness of her mother's tendency toward drama, is still likely to believe what her mother tells her.) Also, tonight is Charlotte Anne's turn to exit the stage in the actual horse-drawn carriage with her mother, the Rodolfo, and Dante DiMedici in it, this combination of the short-statured, non-gender-choosing, possibly psychic DiMedici and the carriage ride (chaperoned and public as it was) being more than enough to distract her from the covert and irrevocable meltdown taking place in her bodice.

Onstage, Dante DiMedici pushes his way upstage through the Urchins (ever so slightly brushing against Charlotte Anne in the process, which brushing she will interpret through the end of fourth grade) for his solo. Charlotte Anne imagines that Dante DiMedici is dedicating his solo to her (*"Vo' la tromba, il cavallin!"* Roughly: "Want a trumpet, want a horse!"), that he may be expressing, via the superficial desire of his character (Ragazzo), his own secret passion for Charlotte Anne, that he is, in a way, publicly acknowledging his tenderness for her, and that the audience present at the New York State Theater tonight is able to perceive this subtle message of love and therefore collectively experiences this performance of *La Bohème* as having particular depth and significance. At no time during this solo does Dante DiMedici actually look at Charlotte Anne, but due to her growing certainty about their psychic connection, she does not find this troubling. As they exit in the carriage, Charlotte Anne pictures around her a sea of bleeding soldiers amid the burning of Atlanta as she descends the buggy, nobly tearing off her green velvet costume and its petticoats to fashion into bandages (in this fantasy there is of course no chocolate-covered thin-mint stain, or if there is, the bleeding soldiers seem to pay it no mind) and therefore making more than a good impression upon Dante DiMedici, still in the carriage in imaginary war-torn Atlanta, awestruck at her Scarlett O'Hara–like heroic actions. In reality, what happens with Charlotte Anne's petticoats is that they spill over into Dante DiMedici's lap, and as she tries to contain the wayward garments into her own lap (even though it's a small carriage and Charlotte Anne, her mother, the Rodolfo, and Dante DiMedici are squeezed together in a way that certainly doesn't trouble her at all [and seems not to be troubling to the Rodolfo either, similarly pressed against her mother] even though she cannot actually feel the contact between Dante and herself, the knowledge of the contact is enough for her), Dante whispers to Charlotte Anne, "It's okay," as the carriage moves offstage, confirming in her mind all earlier suspicions as to any possible feelings/psychic connection taking place.

The melted thin mint is finally discovered, of course, as Charlotte Anne changes back into her own dress, and an attempt is made to wash off the offending deep brown stain with cold water and a gooey, gray, communal bar of soap, to little avail, so the soiled undergarments are hung folded underneath the remaining stain-free slip and left next to a brown velvet costume on the rack in the hope that it might be associated with the brown-velvet-wearing urchin (#5) and not herself. (Charlotte Anne has no particular bad feelings for Urchin #5 or anyone, really, for that matter, but is so unprepared for any possible consequences of having stained the petticoats, having an exaggerated fear of getting in trouble wildly disproportionate to the amount of trouble she actually gets in, ever, causing her to worry less about any possible trouble brought about by getting someone else in trouble, in the hope that that person does not have any similarly overexaggerated fear of getting, or being, in trouble, and of course also, that the extent of the trouble would be limited to some appropriate punishment here at the opera house and not both here at the opera house and at home; it's a long way from her mind to think of suggesting that she dry-clean something [she knows what a dry cleaner is, to be sure, but will grow up and still never find out what "Martinizing" means], because, again, she's eight, and this is the sort of logical thing that you figure out with time and experience, and think is an unsolvable problem when you are only eight.) The dresser will make a disdainful comment at a later performance upon noticing the stain, but as it turns out, accusations are never made because of the rotating casts and also the rotating petticoats. Charlotte Anne, age eight, concerned about castration, thumbs through a tattered *Good Housekeeping* during the brief speculation about the chocolate-covered-thin-mint stain, and the speculation turns to boisterous gossip about "someone's" mother "getting it on" with the Rodolfo, which thankfully goes far and above over her head, not only because she's eight but because she's still thinking about Dante and the chocolate-covered thin mint.

Howard the Filmmaker

SO THIS GUY CAME UP TO ME as I was leaving work and he said, *My name is Howard Blah Blah Blah and I'm a filmmaker and I'd like you to be in my new film,* and I said, *Do I look like I was born yesterday?* Granted it probably wasn't the best response I could have come up with considering I was twenty-four and I probably did look like I was born a lot more recently than that guy, anyway. I don't know if he thought I was from Iowa or what, my parents were born there, it's not a total stretch, but I'm a New Yorker, and creepy guys have been coming up to me on the street since I was about eight, and I'll tell you right now I would probably have said the same thing then. Ha.

So where was I. The *filmmaker* went on to tell me that he was in fact totally legitimate (his word) and handed me a piece of paper with his number and said he guaranteed that the video store I just walked out of would have half a dozen of his films. Already I knew by the way he kept using the word *film* about every nine seconds that he somehow thought that being a *filmmaker* entitled him to also be a pervert.

So anyway, I took his number, and he kept talking, and I was standing there like, *uh huh,* not saying much but trying to give him a look that said, "You don't really think I'm *that* stupid," while simultaneously, you know, not walking away. I wasn't an actress.

18

Well, I had thought about it briefly during a rough spot in college. And I do impressions of people, but not for a career. Actually, I was working in the video store. The filmmaker kept talking and in between elaborating on his legitimacy as a filmmaker he made a point of nodding at my limited responses with his eyelids open really wide undoubtedly to convey his sensitive listening skills but which really only made him look like he just put in eyedrops. So he got in a cab and I went back into the store and looked him up on the computer and it turned out that although he was not a porn director, which is frankly what he looked like to me, not that I'd ever seen a porn director, but if I were to come up with my best guess about what a porn director looked like, it could easily be a fat bald guy with a big scar on one eyelid that makes him look like he's perpetually leering, which I'm going to guess was fitting in his case, anyway, I looked him up and there were a whole bunch of movies listed there, not in the porn section, none of which I'd ever seen although I did remember hearing of a couple of them.

So I took home *Wolf Diaries* and *The Addict* and as it turned out I have to amend my comment about him not being a porn director because frankly, there were sex scenes in both those films that were so vile I thought about telling my boss to put them in the back of the store. And both of them featured this Howard guy which trust me is not something you should ever have to pay money to see. It became pretty clear, watching these *films*, that Howard the film-maker was both the wolf and the addict, and that he should also make a movie called *Denial* because the wolf and the addict are both played by the same very handsome quirky actor who in no way resembled Howard the filmmaker. There are also sex scenes aplenty featuring the handsome quirky actor that aren't any more palatable just because the actors are better-looking. There's not an awful lot of dialogue, and I haven't seen a lot of porn but it seemed like only the most marginal step up. These people were talking about their *feelings* and that sort of thing, as opposed to describing their boners or whatever, but really it still seemed like filler between the sex scenes. But both the movies are cut in such a way as to give the appearance of making some *artistic statement*, and you just know Howard the filmmaker was simultaneously going to people, *Hey, look at me, look what I did with the lighting,* while thinking to himself, *That actress looks really hot with my dick up her ass.* Which, trust me, she really doesn't.

Nevertheless I was possessed to call him for reasons I can't entirely explain, although when he asked, I couldn't really bring myself to make any comment about his *work* that wouldn't be completely rude, and he told me to meet him at the Pierre for lunch. I don't know what I was thinking, really. At that point, I was pretty much thinking "lunch." I don't really eat at places like the Pierre on a regular basis. I tried to find something in my closet that someone would wear to the Pierre for lunch, which ended up being the itchy skirt from a wool suit that my mother had bought me for interviews that I never went on and a pink-and-gray sweater that had a lot of pills at that point and I ended up looking like, I don't know what, someone who was neither me nor someone who goes to the Pierre for lunch. I got there and he waved me over while he was talking on a telephone someone had obviously brought over (which I gathered from the inane conversation was solely for the purpose of indicating to me that supposedly important filmmakers take calls on phones that people bring over) and he was seriously saying to the person, *And what did you think of the part where he's rubbing his penis against her ass crack?* Those were his actual words, he said *ass crack* like that right in front of me. *Did you find that believable?* he went on, *Did you find that to be arousing? And disturbing, good, good . . .* , and then he covered the phone and said to me, *I'll be done in a second,* and then finished up his conversation about whoever's penis and ass crack as though he was talking about some cereal he had for breakfast or something. Then he told me to order whatever I wanted so I ordered filet mignon and then he took another penis call and finally got off the phone for a full two minutes so he could tell me this long involved story about the wild life he'd led back in the seventies living with some quarterback and having big druggy sex parties all the time which I gathered anyone present was invited to participate in and I was sitting there nodding not enjoying my filet mignon as much as I could, thinking of him in an orgy while also trying to act as unshocked as possible because it seemed obvious to me that that's what he was looking for. Either that or you know, *Whoop de do, let's go get a room.* So then he took another phone call and this time he got up from the table and carried the phone away with him while he was talking like he had something more private to say than *ass crack* and didn't come back until I was almost finished with this very tall chocolate raspberry dessert and he said, *So what did you think of that story I told you?* To which I said, *You know, I'm not an actress, and therefore I am not interested in having sex with you.* Just like that, I said that, I really did. And he said, *Oh, no, that's cool, sometimes it happens, sometimes it doesn't, I'm just really looking for someone who understands the work, someone who . . . you just strike me as having the intelligence that this character needs.* And then he told me that the same quirky actor I happened to love would be my co-star. So then he's mind-fucking me, right, both because who wouldn't want to co-star with that guy and also because he must have perceived, somehow, that this was my weak spot, people thinking I'm stupid. Which I'm not. I didn't go to Harvard like Howard the filmmaker, who at age like, fifty or whatever he is, managed to remind me about six times that he went to Harvard while I was just thinking, Man, you were in the class of '47 or something, give it a fucking rest. I work in a video store. Someone says he wants to put me in a movie who actually makes movies, even if they are bad, you know, fine, put me in a movie. Anything would have been better than alphabetizing gay porn. So he gave me a script and told me he wanted me to read for the part of Angeline but if I was more compelled by another character he'd love to see what I did with that too.

So I went home and the script was about this good-looking young filmmaker, it was actually called *Henry the Filmmaker*, just in case old Howard hadn't said that word enough times, who's kind of hypersexed but of course really wants true love, and he goes around trying to seduce all these women he sees on the street, while at the same time also pursuing the elusive one he really cares about, who of course does have sex with him but that detached kind of sex where she's not emotionally involved with him at all which in my opinion was the real fantasy of Howard the film-maker. And of course there's the obligatory cameo in which old Howard, something of a mentor to his younger alter ego, has sex with a young novice in a church basement while Henry looks on taking notes or jerking off or something. What that has to do with filmmaking I'm not sure. The only thing that's even a little bit believable about this movie is that the young filmmaker is considerably more handsome than Howard the old fat bald filmmaker and therefore you could see where maybe one or two random women who only just met him on the street might ever want to have sex with him. Otherwise it veers off into some weird netherworld where the woman has this compulsive gambling problem even though by day she's a prim schoolteacher and she gets deeper and deeper into the debt of the gambling problem until eventually the young filmmaker is the only person who can possibly help her or relate to her because he obviously has this compulsion of his own, but then it's still kind of a thing where in the end even though she's shed a very dramatic tear out of her left eye she's still kind of detached which allows Henry the filmmaker to be left kind of perpetually pursuing her which again is a very nice fantasy coming from a sex addict. He kind of gets to have it both ways.

Anyway there were all these small parts, and the one he wanted me to read for, Angeline, is this novice who the old wise filmmaker has some really nasty sex with, to which I said one more time, *I'm not an actress.* I didn't need to do shit like that for my art. I had no art. So I called him up and told him so, and I was thinking I could write a better script than that in my sleep, but since the last thing I'd written was a fuck-off letter to my last boyfriend a year before, I said, *I'll read for the part of Marie,* this woman on a bus in a fur coat who tells the young filmmaker to go fuck himself after he asks if he can stick his fingers inside her fur. So he said, *That's fine, meet me in the lobby of the Pierre at 11:00.* At night.

I have no explanation for why I went except I wasn't the least bit worried that I couldn't kick his own ass crack if I needed to. But then I got there and he said, *Come up to my room,* and I was like, one more time, *I'm not an actress, I'm not going to sleep with you for something I truly don't care about.* Which I realize now might have given him the impression that I would have fucked him if he'd had something to offer that I did care about. I didn't say it right, but thankfully he didn't come up with a counteroffer, he just said, *That's fine, I really think you have an interesting quality that would translate well on film,* and I was just like, all right already, let's get this over with, and we went up to this huge suite and he read the part of the young filmmaker and said his icky line which truly wasn't even necessary at that point in order for me to find the motivation to tell him to fuck off, and he took a meaningful deep breath, trying to show me how impressed he was with my natural acting talent. He said, *That was really powerful.* And I just thought, Oh please. Even though I know I was kind of convincing, he would have said that no matter what I did. So anyway then he said some stuff about financing and locations and dropped some names and said they were just in the early stages but he'd get in touch with me when they were ready to go into production even though he hadn't taken my number and I didn't really want to give it to him anyway. I figured he knew where I worked and he could find me if he wanted to.

So then a year went by and I didn't hear from him which was no big surprise although I did see him in front of the OTB a couple of times looking at racing forms but I always crossed the street before he saw me. Then one day he came into the video store with a bunch of people and I said hi like he was just another customer and he looked at me like he knew me and was wondering if he'd had sex with me but he wasn't exactly sure and so finally I said, *I read for the woman in the fur coat,* and he said, *Right, right, well we're just scouting locations for a different film now, that project you read is in turnaround but I definitely still want you and in the meantime this new film is a documentary I'm sure you'd be fantastic in.* At that point I was just thinking, Don't say *turnaround* to me, and he still didn't take my number but about a week later I saw him in front of the OTB and it was too late to cross the street and he said, *Come up to my apartment right now I want to show you some of the footage we've got on the documentary,* and I said, *That's okay,* and he said, *I live right around the corner, I really want your opinion,* and I was just like, *Why?* and he said he could tell that I saw things that everyone didn't see and I just wanted to go, *So then you know that I see that you're full of shit, right?* but apparently I was worried about offending him, so I said, *I have to be somewhere in a half hour* (which I really didn't), and he said, *That's fine,* and I realized from the bizarre half-formed grin on his face that he probably wanted to say he could do it six times in a half hour but for some reason decided to restrain himself. So I went up to his apartment and thankfully there was a housekeeper there and he put a tape in the VCR and it was basically just him interviewing all different kinds of people about sex, pretty much anything they felt like saying about sex or if they happened to feel like engaging in sex with him while the camera continued to roll. I watched a segment in which he asks this one woman if she shaves her pubic hair and she says that she does and he asks her why she does that and she says she thinks it's erotic or something and he says to her casually but all Mr. Intellectual Feminist Prick, *So you don't find that to be an insult to your womanhood,* like it's this important opinion he heard someone say but you could tell he couldn't give a shit one way or another and sure enough in the next second he tells her exactly what he wants to do to her clean-shaven pussy and when it looks like she's about to let him I was just like, okay, *Gotta go,* and he said, *Did that make you uncomfortable?* and I said, *If you mean by uncomfortable did it make me feel like I might throw up, then yes,* and he said, *So if I told you right here, right now what I wanted to do to you would that make you uncomfortable?* and as his fat hand came toward my face as though there was any chance that he perceived some kind of agreement on my part which wasn't there, I pushed it away from me and I said, *I am not interested in you,* and he said, *Not even a little? You came up here,* and I said, *Get away from me, you're hideous,* which he is, and he said, *Well Carmela didn't think so when she was masturbating me in my bed last night, isn't that right, Carmela?* he said in the direction of the housekeeper who nodded but who obviously didn't speak enough English to dispute his claim and who couldn't possibly have been doing anything the night before other than praying to the Lord Jesus to save her fat-assed fucking perverted boss from the depths of hell. Then I slammed the door behind me without saying goodbye.

I'm not an actress, I already said that. It was naïve of me to think that this guy would give me a part based on my having an intelligent quality and probably he wouldn't have given me a part even if I did have sex with him. But I'm a little bit older now, and I really don't want to work in a video store for the rest of my life as you can well imagine, who would, and my friends all seem to agree that my impressions are totally right on. So I think I'm going to go spend a little time in Hollywood and see what happens. Howard the filmmaker said I could use his name.

✦

Perversion #1:
The Beautiful Crissy Experience

✦

CHARLOTTE ANNE BYERS, age nine, has only been in New York for a little over three years, but she already knows too much. Lesson Number One: Ditch the southern accent. Charlotte Anne arrived in the city, practically in white gloves ("Always dress up for the airplane," her mother said), only weeks before her first-grade debut in the New York City public school system, where she learned in a matter of days to discard the southern accent, thankfully, via the experience of her classmate Sue Ellen Smiley, whose combination drawl/unfortunate surname made her the target of endless ridicule. It would be a while before Charlotte Anne was able to completely stop using the phrase "Y'all," but minus the accent, it didn't seem to damage her socially in any significant way. (One kid insisted on calling her "Byer Self" and tried to bring the name into wide usage, but he had to explain the joke too many times and it never caught on.) With regard to her friend Karen Pink-Park, who has a surprisingly strong sense of herself in spite of her petite stature, and is not cursed in Smiley fashion by her unusual last name (in fact, she thinks it's cute), attempts have been made at abuse, but Karen, who is quite pretty, has a way of squinting her eyes that will sufficiently frighten any child enough to cause them to consider seriously what she was capable of doing, post-squint. Karen, who was part of Charlotte Anne's small circle by the beginning of third grade, is generally willing to overlook the presence of an occasional "Y'all." Karen Pink-Park has other things on her mind.

Lesson Number Two: A fire drill is when you exit the school building in an orderly fashion so you know what to do in case of fire. A schoolwide assembly is held the first week of school each year for the purpose of talking about fire safety (at which assembly most of the fifth-grade class is already kind of bored, since they've heard it all five times, snickering among themselves that they should have a Charlie Chop Off Drill or an Evil Babysitter Drill, referring to one probably mythical criminal who chopped off little boys' parts and one entirely real crime in which the sister of a girl whose birthday party Charlotte Anne had once been to was kidnapped and subsequently brutally murdered and left in a trash can). Charlotte Anne and most of her classmates feel reassured by the friendly firemen and their explanations and advice, probably in some way indirectly contributing to Lesson Number Three: Don't ask about the civil defense drill. Nine-year-old Charlotte Anne, in New York for a little over three years, still has no idea what the words *civil* or *defense* mean, together or separately, why no friendly civil defensemen come to assemble and inform, or why the civil defense alarm (something like a totally deafening police siren) is considerably more frightening than the fire alarm (more like a really noisy bicycle bell). Charlotte Anne knows only that when the totally deafening civil defense alarm goes off, you are to exit the classroom in an orderly fashion but remain in the hallway, lined up with your back to the wall, crouched, knees to shoulders, arms over head.

Charlotte Anne also knows that all kids don't keep their Beautiful Crissy dolls (with the beautiful, "growing" hair) as pristine as she would, if she had one, that there are kids who cut their dolls' hair, or lose parts of games, and that some of them will invite you over for a playdate saying that they have a certain game and then that turns out to be a lie, or don't know where they even keep things, which she will usually consider when invited over for a playdate, seeing as how what's the point, really, if there are only parts of things to play with. Charlotte Anne decides to go over to play with Karen Pink-Park and especially to see Karen's new brunette Beautiful Crissy, only to discover that this Beautiful Crissy has only a sort of pixie cut, not unlike the one on her own head she's still growing out, the one her mother said would look "so cute" (but mostly seemed to be about cutting off all the blonde parts from a previous occasion when she had bleached her daughter's naturally brown hair, also executed with the "so cute" reasoning) that coincided with the move to New York and the curious absence of her dad (Charlotte Anne has never heard anyone besides her friend Meg Davidson say the word *divorce*, will not hear the word said by an adult until sometime later in third grade when her mother tells her "the divorce is final" with few additional details and with Charlotte Anne not asking any questions, since she learned from Meg Lesson Number Four: Divorce is when your dad moves to someplace called Encino because it's cheaper to start a handbag business there), which unfortunate combination of events served mostly to mark the time when she started making mental notes on things in New York not seeming quite right. In addition to the unfortunate haircut, Charlotte Anne also notices that the hole in the Crissy doll's head where the ponytail is supposed to "grow" from is empty, exposing the spool around which the ponytail would wrap or unwrap when you pressed in the "belly button," depending on whether you were "growing" or "putting back" the ponytail. (Charlotte Anne is increasingly bothered by a literal view of the Crissy doll's hair-growing, as she also knows that she has neither a spool inside her head nor a belly button that activates anything, and thinks of writing a letter to the Ideal company suggesting that they make some more realistic and possibly educational growing apparatus.) Charlotte Anne is not the sort of kid who would ever ask another kid why they would do such a thing, especially not Karen Pink-Park, who was likely to offer a scary squint. And so when Charlotte Anne thoughtlessly says, "Let's do something else," she's not really thinking that Karen is going to say she wants to talk about boys, which Charlotte Anne is neither interested in nor knows anything about. Which explains her answer to Karen Pink-Park's question, "If a boy wanted to see this, or this," pointing to higher and lower portions of her anatomy, "what would you show him?" Charlotte Anne doesn't think to realize this is an unlikely scenario, or that she could maybe say, "That's kind of a yucky question," which is what she thinks but would never say, not sure if everyone is possibly going to move to Encino if she says the wrong thing, and so instead says, trying to sound casual, "This," pointing to the pockets of her pants, which is as close as she wants to get to pointing to anything else. Charlotte Anne has been accumulating some

useful information since the move north, but not included is anything regarding to what these parts do, only the knowledge that
there's some good reason why you try to keep them covered up.
"No," Karen advises, "you show him this," she says, pointing to her
shirt. Karen Pink-Park has a tone of voice that defies challenge, even
to someone who might be inclined, which Charlotte Anne is not.
Karen looks bored. "Let's go bounce on my sister's bed."

Charlotte Anne and Karen make their way through a long hallway to her sister Sunny's room. Sunny has a four-poster canopy
bed that captures Charlotte Anne's imagination, that she files away
on her mental list of things that other girls have. Sunny Pink-
Park, not nearly as cute as her older sister, is never given a choice
about the bed-bouncing, and is also about as far away from any
metaphoric representation of her given name as possible, and by
the end of the afternoon, Charlotte Anne will have a pretty good
idea that Sunny may not have initially started out her life looking
so gloomy and not sunny. Charlotte Anne and Karen jump up and
down on Sunny's bed while Sunny kind of slumps over her desk
ignoring them, doodling some frowny-faces on her math home-
work and drawing a self-portrait in the margins, in which frowny-
faced Sunny is holding an umbrella directly underneath a big sun.
Karen tries to make a game out of who can touch the canopy the
most times, which isn't a feat of any kind for either of them, even
the shorter Karen, and Charlotte Anne is aware that Karen has a
thing about winning, and that it's better just to let her win, even in
a dumb game the rules of which, Charlotte Anne notices, keep
changing in order to create a more favorable outcome for Karen.

Some minutes after the bouncing game begins, Charlotte Anne realizes that Karen and Sunny's father has been standing in the doorway watching, and stops jumping for a minute, because at her house, anyway, bouncing on the bed leads to no TV. "It's okay," Karen Pink-Park's dad says, with a smile that makes Charlotte Anne uncomfortable enough to decide she's tired of bouncing without knowing exactly why, and Karen bounces off the bed right around the same time. "I'm going to the deli," the dad says. "Mom needs milk. I'll bring you back something." Sunny Pink-Park rolls her eyes.

Karen doesn't wait but a second to bring Charlotte Anne into her parents' room, opening the door to a walk-in closet lit by a bare bulb attached to a long string. Karen Pink-Park turns on the light, revealing Karen/Charlotte Anne–high stacks of a newspaper called *Screw* lining the walls of the closet. "He sits in here," Karen says casually. "Look," she adds, pointing to a cover illustration of a man and a woman, undressed in what appears to be some kind of lap-sitting arrangement. Charlotte Anne finds this to be a thoroughly repulsive image, and decides it's time to go home.

The following week, Charlotte Anne's friend Meg Davidson invites her over for a playdate, and Charlotte Anne, who knows there's some weirdness over at the Davidsons' too, thinks it's a better weirdness, and overlooks the cockroaches and the openly pot-smoking mom ("It's just a roach," Meg says, naturally causing Charlotte Anne to question the smoking of bugs, but still not being as openly creepy as Karen Pink-Park's dad's bounce-spectating and *Screw* magazines). Meg also has a Beautiful Crissy doll that

Charlotte Anne is interested in, even though she correctly suspects that Meg's Beautiful Crissy will also have a non-working ponytail. In fact, Meg's Beautiful Crissy does have a pixie cut similar to Karen Pink-Park's Beautiful Crissy, except for Meg's Beautiful Crissy's pixie cut has also been painted blue. (Meg Davidson's mother is an artist and encourages this sort of activity, which blue doll–painting Charlotte Anne knows for sure would not result in any kind of praise at her house but might possibly result in her mother moving to Encino.) Charlotte Anne knows it's just a matter of time before the blue-haired Beautiful Crissy becomes part of Meg Davidson's "doll sculptures," a series of "works," Meg calls them, in which mostly naked dolls and/or doll parts are glued together into big piles, and sometimes painted or sprinkled with glitter. Next to each sculpture is a 3×5 card with little titles Meg wrote on them, such as RED DOLL PILE, like Charlotte Anne has seen next to the paintings at the museum. Since the Beautiful Crissy experience at Meg's is also unsatisfying, Meg and Charlotte Anne have an afternoon of painting the hallway whatever color(s) they feel like, and when Charlotte Anne's mother arrives, the girls whine that they've just put on a Beatles record, so her mother says to Meg, "Enjoy, I'll go catch up with your mom," which statement is curious in and of itself, since at home, on the rare occasion that anything besides classical music is audible, her mother will invariably say, "I don't know what that is, but it's not music." Charlotte Anne, age nine, has found this alliance of mothers peculiar from the beginning, given their divergent tastes in music *and* aesthetics (Charlotte Anne's mother not being likely, at any given moment, to paint her bedroom walls black, or orange, and for sure not to let her paint the hall), nevertheless her mother disappears into Meg's mother's black bedroom from which room some giggles and whoops can be heard even over the kind of loud *Rubber Soul*. During the hall-painting Charlotte Anne mentions to Meg that she's been over to Karen Pink-Park's house for a playdate. Meg sticks out her tongue and says, "Her dad's such a creep. He once showed me his dick and asked me to rub powder on it." Charlotte Anne has never heard the word *dick* before, has not had any kind of "talk" with her mother yet, but suddenly has a very visual image in her mind of an extraneous part she had noticed on the cover of the *Screw* magazine that hadn't been of particular appeal to her, which she also recognized as a part she didn't have. Charlotte Anne, curious and repulsed to know the outcome but more concerned about being rude, doesn't ask what happened, but the barely concealed look of horror on her face causes Meg to say, "Ew, I didn't do it. Didn't your mom tell you not to touch some guy's dick when he puts it in your face?"

"Sure she did," Charlotte Anne says, wondering why she didn't, not considering that maybe her mother wouldn't think there was any reason to say such a thing to a fourth grader, that this wouldn't be anything she'd need to worry about, really, although there was that Charlie Chop Off the bigger kids kept talking about. Charlotte Anne's mother comes out of the black bedroom looking sort of sleepy, and pats her daughter on the head with a limp hand. "Time to go, honey," she says. "Bye, Meggie," she says, waving the floppy hand behind her. Charlotte Anne will end up never seeing a fully functional Beautiful Crissy doll and will grow up and never find out if the Charlie Chop Off story was real or a tall tale, but the thing about Karen Pink-Park's dad seemed realer, and kind of even creepier, and she adds all of it to her list of mental notes, for future reference.

Famous

AROUND THE NEIGHBORHOOD, there are people who are kind of famous, and I'm one of them. We're not like movie stars, just people you see sort of *around*, all the time, either where we work or just even on the street. I wait tables at a sort of upscale pizza joint on the corner of 81st and Amsterdam called Pie. (Not a very well-thought-out name, although the owners don't like to admit that out loud, but the fact is that a lot of people come in asking for pie and then leave when they find out it isn't apple.) I didn't realize I was one of the famous people until this guy came up to me on the street one day and said, *You!* sort of accusingly, and for a second I seriously thought I'd done something to him, except then he goes, *You're that girl, from the pizza place.* I didn't recognize him as a regular or anything, but I was relieved as soon as I realized his tone was friendly, and then finally he said, *I have wanted to meet you for the longest time.* And I didn't want to be rude, but all I could think to say was, *Why?* I don't mean to be naïve. I'm cute enough. I wear a short denim skirt, and the blue t-shirt we wear definitely brings out my eyes. And I know there's a waitress thing, for some guys. But that second, I thought, Okay, so you think I'm cute, but how do you know I'm not a terrible person? I felt like he put me in some place that was different than him.

I never saw him at Pie again after that. I probably made him feel bad.

Anyway, like I said, there are other famous neighborhood people, like the bartender from KCOU next door, Mike, who every night gets a scoop of vanilla ice cream with hot fudge to go, and this creepy guy with those kind of giant glasses that make your eyes look blurry, like they're not even there; he's tall but kind of hunches over and leaves twenty-five-cent tips no matter what, and is apparently outside at all times. I see him every day. He knows a lot of people, or vice versa, and it doesn't seem like he could possibly have a job, but I'm sure he's not homeless either. Or he's like, a homeless mover and shaker. Then there's Mary, who *is* homeless, who wears two pairs of glasses taped together and complains about the food we give her for free. You hand her a take-out container and she says, *I hope this doesn't have too much pepper like last time.* At Pie, the owners are all pretty famous too, seven Italian brothers and sisters, the most famous being the youngest, identical twin brothers. I have sort of an on-again off-again thing with the middle brother, but really, we don't have a lot in common. I think it's just for the purposes of trying to get into his family. I'm an only child. Well, I have steps, but they live in Iowa.

There are a lot of regulars at Pie, some of whom actually are famous away from the Upper West Side, and some of whom are famous except I had no idea who they were until one of the sisters told me. This one cute guy came in a lot and would always wave to me when he walked by. *That's Declan Reed,* the sister said. I nodded like she was just telling me his name, which obviously made her realize I was missing something, because she said, *Declan Reed. From*

The Basement. He lives in the basement? I asked. *No, Charlotte, the band, The Basement.* I wasn't really a fan or not a fan of The Basement. They're sort of the Philadelphia version of Bon Jovi, but not so focused on hair. Anyway, one day he came in and I said, *I didn't know you were in The Basement,* and he said, *And when you found out, were you just like, he lives in The Basement? Pretty much,* I said, and he laughed, and he started coming around a little more often and then one of his bandmates came in with him and was just like, *Dude totally wants to go out with you and is afraid to ask.* Declan nodded indicating the truth of it and somehow we ended up making plans without either of us exactly asking the other out.

On our so-called date, we had lunch at Peretti's and he asked me stuff like, *Who are you? Where are you from? What do you think about god?* I'm not sure anyone really has the time to hear my feelings about god, which are muddled at best, but I love that someone asked, anyway. Afterward we walked around Central Park for a while even though it was a little drizzly, and he held my hand, and I did like him, although did you ever have an experience when someone was holding your hand but it was just sort of, not necessarily romantic? Practically the first thing he told me about himself was that he'd just broken up with someone, and he told me more about it than I might have needed to know, you know, private things that maybe he could just as well have explained to me in the abstract, which isn't unusual though, guys talk to me, I don't know why, and generally I don't mind talking about anything except romantically it's not so good to really like someone who's just gotten out of a relationship. Although he did get cuter and cuter, because he was obviously really smart, graduated from Penn with an art degree, and he was very funny, and those are two things that always make someone much cuter to me. The second thing he told me was that he was in therapy, and that he was an alcoholic, and that he had been in A.A. for four years, which I thought was cool and all for him, but also kind of fascinating. I knew that there were a lot of cool people in A.A., but I just couldn't really imagine someone not ever drinking again. It seemed kind of extreme. The third thing he told me was that he hated his job. And I thought, Okay, maybe you're not in the coolest band in the world, but I think I could stand trading places with you.

So anyway, we got to be really good friends, and nothing romantic ever did come of the hand-holding, which was fine with me. I was still on-again off-again with the brother and Declan was still preoccupied with his ex, who he was also on and off with. I thought he'd given me quite a number of details about the ex-girlfriend until it came out that she was a model (which, I have to say, is information I rarely want to have) and that she had graduated from the Sorbonne when she was, I dunno, eight (meaning she was super smart as well as being a model), and that she was nineteen. When they broke up. And apparently, at least when he first told me this, her age had nothing to do with it. I guess I maybe didn't mention that Declan Reed is forty. I'm only twenty-six myself, but you know, okay, whatever. He looks younger and theoretically I feel like it shouldn't matter but twenty-one years seemed like a lot. It wasn't like I thought he had it all sewn up, that's for sure, but I think sometimes older people think they have it all sewn up when the truth is they're not even near the machine, which is its own kind of problem.

Declan was always talking about *issues,* and some of his more obvious ones were kind of hard to deal with, and you know, fine, everyone in New York goes to therapy at one time or another but he was very into telling me about certain particular issues, like his lust, while also being very into exhibiting other particular issues he seemed to be unaware of. For example, he would describe certain behaviors of his as being *classically alcoholic,* he called it, e.g., obsessing about people, or obsessing about anything (which also describes everyone I know), or doing anything more than is commonly considered normal. Like let's say we go into a record store, I'll put one record in my basket, actually I don't really even take a basket, and he'll put seriously about fifteen in his basket and then he'll pay for mine too. (I certainly don't hate that habit, but I mean, I don't take advantage of it either, which I'm sure is part of why he likes me.) Or you know, he'll eat Chinese food every single day for a week. Well, guess what, I've been eating Froot Loops for breakfast every single day since forever. I'm pretty sure I don't need to examine the deeper meaning of that. Once I made the mistake of saying that Johnny Depp came into the Pie and I made him an ice cream cone, and I didn't even have a chance to say how gorgeous he was (which he was) before Declan seriously grilled me on exactly how gorgeous he was, and in what way, and was he as good-looking as Johnny Depp (is anyone?) like a dog that will just not let go of a bone. The whole conversation was all about me reassuring Declan that he too was incredibly handsome — I also reminded him that he had the whole rock star thing as a bonus, and that I didn't see any girls throwing their bras at Johnny Depp or anything — as many compliments as I could come up with.

But then it would come up again and again, how his hairline was receding (it wasn't) and in what way, or should he get a tattoo to seem younger (what kind of rock star asks anyone else if he should get a tattoo?), or could I see his crow's-feet (no). And then after I convinced him as sincerely as possible that he didn't need to do any of those things, he asked me to tell him which of his features were my favorite. I actually participated in this for a while. I told him that his eyebrows were truly underrecognized. Later on I was just like, *Okay, we're not doing that today.*

He told me he wanted to go solo, and do a totally different kind of music. More of a James Taylor kind of thing, except he wasn't really like James Taylor at all, and anyway, he often made a big point of saying that the record industry pigeonholed you into this or that, and that he couldn't get a break (which I don't really agree with, anyway, I think you can always be the exception to that kind of thing), even though he was very rich and every single time we went out people asked him for his autograph and once we were holding hands and this girl grabbed his other hand and yanked him over to her so hard that I fell into a potted palm and bruised my knee and you can be sure she didn't say she was sorry. But actually I kind of felt even worse for him that time, because he just won't be rude to these people, and yet, you know, they take it for granted that they can touch him or whatever. When a stranger on the street touches me I'm like, *Back the fuck up.* Anyway, sometimes he would play songs for me on his acoustic guitar and I'd say, *Oh that was really great,* and he'd say, *Really, you think so?* and I would try to be encouraging to him, but the truth is I'm a very bad liar, and I can't even believe he didn't notice that, although I'm of course glad he didn't. But the lyrics would be something like, *Monique's hair fell down to there, she smoked Gauloises like I breathe air, I really wish I didn't care, didn't care, didn't care* . . . A couple of them were a little better than that and when I sang harmony on the second chorus of one of them he acted as impressed as if I'd discovered plutonium or something. He said, *Do you realize how hard that is? To just pick up a melody and then harmonize?* I said, *Not really*, since it wasn't, but I was thinking that in my family if you didn't have that kind of thing as a basic skill you were probably switched at birth. They're all musicians. Declan told me I had a really beautiful voice and asked why I didn't sing and I said, *I did when I was a kid, and then, I dunno, I'm more into writing screenplays and stuff now.* Admittedly I was stretching it, in my mind there was more of an emphasis on the "and stuff," but I was thinking about writing screenplays, anyway. *Okay, I just got weird about it. Anyway I don't write music.* To which he said, *Oh, it's easy, anyone can write music*, to which I of course out of politeness repressed an urge to say, *Not anyone*, considering how nice he was being to me. Anyway, I said, *I guess it's an issue.*

Right after that, he ran into Monique and they got back together for a while, during which time I assume she took over the job of reassuring him about his hairline not receding and his being better-looking than Johnny Depp and whatever else he was obsessed with that week. Maybe not. Maybe French girls don't do that. In any case, she had apparently just shaved her head, which not only bumped her up into a supermodel, for reasons beyond my grasp (because you can be sure that if I ever shaved my head, not only would I not be able to look at myself but everyone I know would think that something was very seriously wrong, and I seriously doubt I'd get a promotion), it made him even a thousand times more attracted to her. During an off period with the middle brother I was flirting with this preppy kind of Wall Street guy who used to come in after work for a beer and a pizza, always rumpled-looking. Not my type, really, but whatever. I met him at KCOU after my shift and between him and buybacks from the ice-cream bartender, who also didn't drink (what's with that?), I was seriously drunk and went home with him. I have no idea what we could have talked about that led up to this, it wasn't anything I was in the habit of, and I didn't really think we had all that much in common before we went to KCOU, I just thought he was semi-cute. Anyway, we fooled around a little and were on the verge of fooling around a lot, but as soon as he got naked he passed out, and my buzz was starting to wear off, at which time I became extremely grossed out at both the hideousness of his pale naked body and how preppy he was naked even, with like crew socks on, not to mention, you know, that I was there, and I left around four a.m. without even saying anything. I started to write a note and then I just threw it out. I think I was hoping he wouldn't remember. For sure I was hoping I would forget it myself.

Declan came by the next day on the verge of a second breakup with Monique the Model, so we commiserated and I told him the story of the preppy guy (if I knew his name, I'd use it; I'm pretty sure it's Bill — he looks like a Bill, but I can't say that's it for sure) and I realized halfway during the story, when he interjected a similar tale from his drinking days, that he was kind of comparing me to him, like this was *classically alcoholic*, I guess just in case I thought that my drinking had anything to do with it, which I didn't. I mean obviously I wouldn't have gone home with him if I had been sober. I'm just saying I didn't really see how that was alcoholic (actually he may not have said that out loud at all, but it seemed like it was there); everyone does stupid things when they get drunk. Anyway, Monique the Model took up with a woman, which I guess she didn't see as a conflict, but which made Declan's whole self-image thing a gazillion times worse, considering now he wasn't just competing with male models and Johnny Depp but with like, everyone. He seemed kind of different than before though, like he was almost starting to see that he was maybe responsible for choosing, you know, poorly, and he admitted to me that this wasn't the first time he'd been cheated on for a woman and also that maybe the age difference mattered more than he wanted to admit. Then he mumbled something about motives that I didn't really catch and when he left, he looked really blue and kind of like he wasn't in the universe.

Bill, or whatever, did come back to the Pie, and neither of us mentioned anything about his having been naked, and it was hard to tell whether he remembered it or not, but the sight of him made me totally queasy, so I went next door after work and sat and talked to the ice-cream guy for a while. *Mike, are you friends with that guy Bill?* Mike got this grin on his face, like he knew exactly what happened or something, and he said he'd been a friend of Bill's for sixteen years, so I said, *Really? Since Bill was like, a kid?* Then he laughed and said, *Wait, Bill who?* I said, *That preppy guy I was with the other night,* and Mike totally cracked up and explained that in A.A., if someone says they're a friend of Bill's, it's code that they're in the program. I told him I knew this other guy from A.A. and asked him if he thought sleeping with preppy guys was *classically alcoholic* and he said, *The only difference between an alcoholic and everyone else is that we drink too much.* *Okay,* I said, *but how do you know when too much is too much?* Mike laughed again and said, *Well, one way is when your wife leaves the state with no forwarding address.* He could see the wheels turning in my mind, and that this information wasn't helping me personally as any kind of gauge. Not that I was really thinking about it before Declan said those things, anyway. *How about this,* he said. *Shit happens when you drink that wouldn't happen if you didn't.* Well, of course I started reviewing my entire life right then and remembered the time I got lost walking home from a bar that was a block away from my dorm and the time I tried to climb over the White House gates to try to talk some sense into President Reagan and then also the whole almost flunking out of college thing, but I just couldn't get past that image of old men in tattered overcoats who drink all day. I don't even drink every day. He could see I still didn't get it and so he said, *Look, I'm gonna take this beer away from you and give you a soda instead,* obviously to prove a point, and even though there was only about an inch left in the bottle, it still seemed like a waste, but I let him take it away and give me a soda, and you know, it was fine. I had beer at home. I sat there and bullshitted with him for another hour and it was no big deal.

* * *

About a week later Declan came into the Pie, not looking very good, and as soon as I saw him I remembered this terrible dream I had about him just the night before where we were on this old boat, like an old slave ship but without the slaves, and he was seriously drunk and then fell down this flight of rickety wooden stairs and either died or seemed like he died and it was one of those dreams where you're screaming and screaming but no one is really paying much attention. I told him I was so glad to see him but he didn't seem glad about anything right then and when I told him about the dream he said he wasn't surprised because the night before he was driving back from a concert at Giants Stadium and he had been thinking that a really good idea would be to get drunk or drive his car straight into a tollbooth. During the concert some girl tore off her top and jumped on the stage and was hanging all over him for a minute before the bodyguards pulled her off, but anyway I guess she was maybe fourteen or something and he suddenly had this epiphany about Monique the Model, like it was morally wrong, what he'd been doing, that he had to break it off, and that god surely had better plans for him but also somehow he felt like Monique was also responsible, except I didn't quite catch in what way. Something about women and calamity. It didn't make a whole lot of sense, and I felt like he wanted me to just listen and not offer any advice or anything. He said he needed to *work a stronger program,* whatever that meant, and that his behavior with Monique *wasn't in the spirit of love and service* and he just stopped short of saying sex is bad and it almost sounded like he was planning to join the peace corps or something, because there was something really final about it. He thanked me for listening but when we were saying goodbye I went to hug him and he said, *Um, could we not hug?* and I thought, O-kay, *hand-holder,* but I didn't really take it personally, because it was obviously his problem, and I haven't seen him since, except in *People* magazine.

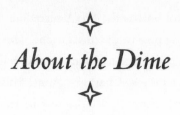

About the Dime

IT DOES NOT OCCUR to her that anyone at LaGuardia might be concerned. At Gate K3, in a crisp flowered dress and matching (and reversible) raincoat (both hand-sewn to perfection by her mother), Charlotte Anne Byers, age nine and a half, hugs her mom goodbye without tears.

About this lack of tears it should be noted:

a) Generally, she is not a big crier
    I) It's been established that there is a one-member-of-the-family-per-household limit on weeping and that that limit has been met
b) She's excited about the trip
c) She's excited about flying by herself, seeing this as further evidence of her independence, which is becoming her trademark
    I) Which she will of course not realize until about thirty years later is not necessarily as useful a quality as she had imagined at age nine and a half.

When the ticket agent announces the boarding of rows ten through twenty-six, Charlotte Anne looks at her boarding pass one more time and boards the TWA plane unaccompanied. C.A. hands her boarding pass to the ticket agent, who escorts her down the tarmac to the plane, and a stewardess shows Charlotte Anne to seat 11A by the window. Charlotte Anne, having flown before (albeit never solo), stows under the seat in front of her a vinyl TWA flight bag filled with the necessary entertainment, including a notebook, a book of games that has answers that get revealed with a special invisible-ink revealing marker (always a little dry), a *Barbie* magazine (subscription copy), one copy of *The Horse on the Roof* (C.A. enjoys any book about city kids), one used and reused copy of *Mad Libs #1* (the funniest thing ever invented), as well as a nightgown (although she's ready to move on to pajamas, as she hates the way nightgowns bunch up) and a toothbrush in case her bags get lost (which will not happen this time but will happen about every other time she flies anywhere in the future), plus also a Betty and Veronica comic book.

About this comic book:

Charlotte Anne is of course pro-Betty, as it is already being established to her that the Veronicas of the world are an obstacle to be overcome, which is arguably a sort of victimy stance for a nine-and-a-half-year-old to be taking and which sort of contradicts the whole independence thing, because why would she even care about/need any Veronicas at all if she were so independent, except for everyone needs a friend, even if they do sometimes try to steal your Archie. Charlotte Anne has formally proposed to Archie Comics that they put out a Betty comic without Veronica, which doesn't happen for several decades but when it finally does happen she will say it was her idea and someone will say to her, *Let it go.*

She buckles her seat belt, pulling it tightly across her lap as instructed, and crosses her legs at the ankle ("Like a lady," her mother has been known to say), trying to tuck her white anklets and loafers as far under her seat as they will go.

About these loafers:

An astute observer might realize they look not only oversized but also not especially feminine; in fact, they were purchased in the men's department at Harry's Florsheim. Charlotte Anne's mother, an opera singer of modest income, a single mom who remembers the depression, is on a budget and reasons that men's shoes are cheaper and that Charlotte Anne has the large feet that run in their side of the family. She is not thinking about the possibility that maybe men's shoes do not do anything to minimize the large size, or that there might be any embarrassment suffered by fourth-grader Charlotte Anne on account of her wearing men's shoes (hence the tucking), there is only a characteristically strange logic, in this case about saving money, that never includes, say, thrift-store girl's shoes, sale shopping, or some similar cost cutting that would result in age/gender-appropriate footwear.

The view from seat 11A is a good one. The weather is clear and she can see the Soldiers and Sailors Memorial in Riverside Park, where she plays frequently with her friend Tracy Corman. Tracy Corman has a pogo stick, which might bump her up into a first-best-friend position were it not for her creepy brother. Charlotte Anne, who knows nothing firsthand of sibling relationships, is pretty sure that at ages nine and eleven, playing hide-and-seek with your clothes off is not a game of hide-and-seek she cares to participate in, plus also Tracy is on the long list of friends who rampantly lop off doll hair and lose parts of games and so there are often few things to do at Tracy's house besides pogo (which turns out to be way less fun in practice than in theory, where C.A. can pogo more than two times before falling over), or play games she has no interest in that don't require game pieces, like naked hide-and-seek. Her experience with siblings thus far has been generally unpleasant; big brothers who hog the TV, little sisters who have never been seen smiling. That said, she thinks she might like to have a sister, not a twin because she thinks twins are creepy, but one who was otherwise pretty much exactly like her, for company.

A stewardess brings Charlotte Anne a pair of wings and a deck of cards and explains that she will be met in Chicago by a TWA representative who will escort her to her connecting Ozark Airlines flight to Cedar Rapids (Charlotte Anne thinks all this personal attention is fabulous until she's about twelve, when she is somehow able to persuade her family to let her find her connecting flight herself, at which time she is already five foot six and can pass for sixteen). Charlotte Anne must have seen an episode of *Hee Haw* or something because she has a lack of confidence about Ozark Airlines she can't exactly place, but puts this aside and arrives in Cedar Rapids slightly late and happy to find that she still recognizes her father. She's seen him exactly one time since she was six.

On the car ride to Iowa City, Charlotte Anne's father talks at some length about Chris and Cal and their games, which he feels C.A. will enjoy. She is not sure who Chris and Cal are but has a vague memory that they might be friends of her grandparents that she hasn't seen for some time and wonders why she's going to be seeing them now. Her father also talks at length about how he met her mother and describes her in a nice way, which is doubly curious as the ensuing physical description does not fit her mother, furthermore it is implied that her mother will be at the house in Iowa City when they arrive, which seems not just unlikely but downright weird.

It turns out that this woman, whose given name is the same as that of Charlotte Anne's mother, is her father's fiancée. (It might be worth noting that her father is both a professor and absent-minded, and has a lifelong habit of forgetting to mention important things like fiancées and [thankfully distant, to date] relatives falling ill or dying. There will also be a time when said absent-mindedness results in forgetting to go for a checkup for seven years, which will cost him a prostate.)

About the name thing:

Charlotte Anne Byers is within a year of being old enough to realize that things like your dad marrying a second woman with the same name or other people in your family having the same name are coincidental. She has one aunt on each side of the family, both named Bonnie, each of whom has two children, a boy and a girl, thus leading Charlotte Anne to the logical conclusion that all kids have two cousins on each side, a boy and a girl, and two aunts named Bonnie. It is not taken into account that Charlotte Anne is herself someone's cousin, but it might be noted that at this point she is not a girl who asks a lot of questions, only one who has them. However weird, in this particular instance, she will come to conclude that if you are divorced and remarry, you must find someone with the same name. This will be cleared up when her mother gets remarried about a year later to a man with his own original name.

Her father's new fiancée has three sons from a previous marriage, Chris, who is her age, Cal, a year older, and Mike, several years older and who appears to be a hippie. (Charlotte Anne has heard about hippies from her mother and it isn't good, but the only identifying clues in this case are Mike's tendency to use the phrase *far out* and his abundant Afro.) Charlotte Anne's future stepmother shows her to her room, where she can unpack. It seems like a better idea to do this immediately than to go downstairs and talk to the three future brothers she had no idea about.

Sewn into the center lining of her eggshell-white Samsonite suitcase is a dime.

About this dime:

This is not any kind of factory mishap or practical joke made by humorously-minded Samsonite workers. The dime has been placed there by Charlotte Anne's mother. Much is made of the dime in the weeks before C.A.'s departure. "It's for a phone call," her mother had said, "in case of emergency." Also sewn into the lining is Charlotte Anne's home phone number (which privately irritates her, as she's known that and her address as well as those of several of her friends and even her old address in Louisiana by heart since first grade). At this point it is nowhere near Charlotte Anne's head that any number of emergencies could arise when she might not be in close proximity to her Samsonite suitcase, for example, let's say she gets mugged waiting in baggage claim. Or gets separated from either one of her parents. Charlotte Anne's mother is thinking of one emergency only. She has reason to believe that Charlotte Anne's father might try to keep her in Iowa, and it does not occur to her that this dime and its location and function, made known to young C.A. Byers in no uncertain terms ("Your father is out to get me," her mother had said, "so if he kidnaps you, all you have to do is find a phone booth and call the police"), might be better located in a lining closer to Charlotte Anne's actual person, say inside her coat, or her dress or shoe even. In fact, C.A. Byers has a ten-dollar bill in her purse as well as thirty-seven cents in loose change with which many calls could be placed and which she is unlikely to lose as she is a particularly responsible nine-and-a-half-year-old, going so far as to point this out to her mother while she was sewing the dime in, to which her mother had said, "This is a whole different thing," and then "Crap," poking herself with the needle due to the inherent awkwardness of trying to sew something into a hard suitcase. The casual tone in which this possible kidnapping/police-phoning had been conveyed is not what reassured Charlotte Anne of her safety, but rather that unlike her mother, Charlotte Anne is not even remotely concerned about her father kidnapping her. (She is, however, somewhat concerned about her mother. She seems a little stressed.) It might be said that outside of the law offices of Stephenson, Lloyd, and Pierce, all communication between her mother and father from 1967–present has been funneled through Charlotte Anne herself. Mostly, her father finds no real reason to communicate with her mother at all (resulting in what will be a protracted resentment in the early part of C.A.'s adulthood; long-distance charges being somewhat prohibitive at this time, the child

Charlotte Anne gets it into her head that he's trying to avoid talking to her mother, and although they will have a large stash of letters and eventually e-mails over the years, Charlotte Anne would like to have heard her dad's actual voice a little more often and will continue to berate him somewhat into his seventies, years after long-distance charges drop significantly), but things like travel plans, while fixed in some ways (according to the custody agreement, every other July/August, every other Easter vacation, every other Christmas vacation), require, at the very least, a communication insofar as flight times and exact dates are concerned which utilizing the United States Postal Service tends to slow down some. That said, Charlotte Anne is never sure how a sentence that begins, "Tell your father . . ." is going to end. It might be "that you are arriving on Ozark flight 257 on the twenty-eighth," and it might be "that I'm tired of these head games." Charlotte Anne has numerous questions about how it might be that her mother and father are playing any kind of games with this decided lack of communication.

Before unpacking anything else, Charlotte Anne takes off the white men's shoes (which will remain in the back of the closet until her return flight home) and removes from her suitcase a pair of red Keds, which she is in the middle of tying when Chris knocks on her open door bearing stickers. "I thought you might want some of these for your door. I had some doubles."

Charlotte Anne takes the Wacky Pack stickers, her favorite, and shuffles through the pile. "I have a bunch of these," she says, handing back an All-Brain Cereal, which she thinks is especially gross anyway.

Chris, apparently unoffended by the lack of a thank-you, which is less about poor manners than poor social skills, takes back the All-Brain, adding, "That one is super gross anyhow, right?" (which as far as C.A. is concerned proves his greatness as a potential brother with whom she has this critical thing in common) and offers to give her any other doubles in the future.

"Your mom lets you put stickers on your door?" she asks her new brother.

He nods and shows her his door, right next to hers. It is covered with stickers. "I have almost all the Wacky Pack first series but I still need a Botch Tape," he says.

"Nobody has Botch Tape," she says.

"I know, right?" The new about-to-be siblings silently contemplate this travesty for a moment by looking down at their shoes. "Look what else." He shows her the inside of the closet he shares with Cal. There's a smaller door inside the closet that goes to the attic. "It's a hideout and junk." Charlotte Anne nods. Secretly she thinks this is the coolest thing ever. The closest thing she has to a hideout is the floor of her closet and a cramped space behind the living-room curtains.

Chris and Charlotte Anne become fast friends, which to nine-and-a-half-year-olds in the early seventies means primarily a shared love of *Brady Bunch* reruns, Wacky Packs, obviously, Mad Libs (although both Chris and Cal are inclined, as boys, to make excessive use of words like *toilet* and *poop*, which aren't all that funny to Charlotte Anne), and anything grape-flavored, although she finds their use of the term *pop* to describe what C.A. refers to as *soda* to be kind of old-fashioned. Additionally, Chris and Cal do have many games and remarkably most of these games have all the needed pieces, due to their mother's diligence about putting things away. But mostly, Chris and Charlotte Anne ride bikes and watch TV and eventually create a somewhat complex society based on spying on her dad. It's meant to be funny, the joke of which is that the kids are spying on/observing the dad's movements and behaviors but which movements and behaviors tend to be innocuous, in fact often there is little or no movement at all, thereby producing what the kids find to be wild humor (a sample from the S.D.W.S. [Secret Dad Watchers Society] minutes: 10:43 a.m. Dad moves paperweight to left of original position. Think: What does this mean?). This society will end up having considerable paperwork and even a treasurer, which somehow Cal agrees to do and ends up financing the entire operation with just under ten of his own dollars, which, when the operation finally disbands (never uncovering anything critical about C.A.'s father), the kids will split equally even though it was Cal's money, with no complaint from Cal. Charlotte Anne, having already seen kids in New York subjected to:

    a) penis-exposing dads
    b) murderous nannies
    c) pot-smoking moms

and

    d) naked brothers

can only conclude that life in Iowa is easy and happy, always, that none of the above would ever happen in such a place, and said conclusions are entered in her notebook for future reference.

About these conclusions, C.A. will discover many years later that kids in Iowa actually and also:

a) smoke pot
b) have sex
c) run away

and also get abused by their parents in a variety of ways just like in every other state, nevertheless when it comes to her attention that Chris had a brief period as a stoner she will be completely stunned and then ask him why he never shared.

Further evidence of the greatness of Iowa living is also noted accordingly. Charlotte Anne's stepmother does laundry and cooks and cleans and goes to Little League games and takes everyone to drive-in movies and to City Park to go swimming (somehow also managing to squeeze in graduate school at the same time) and supplies a bottomless trove of snacks never allowed by her real mother, grape Kool-Aid and candy and gum and huge tubs of ice cream (and chocolate sauce) and Chex Mix and Pop-Tarts any time of the day and when they go to the store she says, "Pick out whatever cereal you like," and Charlotte Anne puts a box of Froot Loops in the cart like she's died and gone to heaven. She learns the "Iowa Corn Song" and sings it often.

It pretty much goes like this for the entire month of July.

Charlotte Anne's father drives her to the airport on July 31 and the plane-boarding scenario is reversed except for Cedar Rapids Airport is pretty small and so she can actually see her dad waving in the terminal from her window on the sixteen-seat plane, which brings us back to the whole tears thing, because although Charlotte

Anne generally keeps such things to herself, a phenomenon occurs whereby she bursts into tears, certain that her father cannot see her waving back, because he keeps waving (about the waving: the Byers side of the family has a thing about waving goodbye to visitors until they are 100 percent certain the visitors are out of sight — it's just what they do, and it will always inspire in Charlotte Anne an uncontrollable urge to burst into tears until she's about thirty-seven and it occurs to her to insist that her dad stop waving because she just can't take it anymore).

So then Charlotte Anne arrives back at LaGuardia and the first thing her mother says to her is, "You've gained weight," and the next time and the time after that her mother will amend this to, "You always gain weight when you go to your father's," making it almost remarkable that the teen/adult Charlotte Anne doesn't have more issues with food than she does, and the truth is that she probably does gain weight on these trips given the extant Willy Wonka universe in Iowa, but another truth is that C.A. Byers is kind of wishing that her mom would just say, "I missed you."

✦

Perversion #2:
Declining the Ken

✦

ALTHOUGH FIFTH-GRADER Charlotte Anne
Byers and her new best school friend (such distinctions being
crucial in assuaging the anxieties of the best day-camp friend, best
in-the-building friend, and all-around/real/true/first best friend),
Rachel Richmond, still play with Barbies, their respective interests
are turning toward other things. Rachel Richmond is trying to figure out how to keep her tube top up and wondering what it would
be like to live in Hollywood. Charlotte Anne is thinking of a
career change. After an impressive early career as an opera singer,
she is beginning to have a stage fright that will ultimately spell the
demise of her operatic career, and sometime during the rehearsals
for P.S. 166's fall production of *The Wizard of Oz*, in which she was
to play the lead role of Dorothy, Charlotte Anne asked to trade
roles with Rachel, who was playing the Cowardly Lion, to no one's
objections. (Charlotte Anne's mother assured her daughter she
respected her decision to decline the lead, although she did casually note in the same breath that Rachel sang out of tune, which in
her household was a crime unequaled by any other atrocities.)
Charlotte Anne has also recently won the school spelling bee and,
as a fortuitous by-product of her having just seen *West Side Story* at

the Regency, first prize in a competition to write a caption for a photo of two pigs kissing ("Maria! I just met a girl named Maria!"), for which she received a check in the sum of ten dollars. Her more recent profession as a child model and actress has been the most short-lived; in spite of her freckle-faced good looks, a local commercial in which she was supposed to slurp up a noodle out of a bowl of soup and say, "It's slurpy delicious," ended in a recast on the first day of shooting due to Charlotte Anne's inability to smile on cue. Fifth-grader Charlotte Anne Byers is not the sort of actress inclined to think about motivation, but without some due cause simply cannot manage more than what comes across on film, apparently, as a knowing closed-mouth smile, which the director naturally felt might be a little disturbing to the population at large who might not want to buy noodle soup from a kid who looked like she maybe knew something about this product, or something about the advertising world, or something about anything a fifth-grader ought not to know something about, not to mention that she was neither a soup-slurper nor the kind of kid who'd use a made-up word unless she made it up herself. The end of her modeling career may be a marginal disappointment to her mother, who spent seventy-five bucks on professional photos, but not any kind of disappointment at all to Charlotte Anne, who, after the success of the pig caption, is more interested in a writing career.

In addition to taking over the role of Dorothy, and of equal importance, Rachel Richmond knows about boys. Fifth-grader Charlotte Anne, who is not necessarily ready to become directly involved with boys, becomes aware that Rachel has some useful information that could help her in the future. (Also, Rachel Richmond's very cool parents invited their daughter's twelve best friends to see the original Broadway production of *Hair* for her tenth birthday [one or two, whose parents felt the material was unsuitable, declined], which cast album Charlotte Anne subsequently begged her mother to drop the four dollars and ninety-nine cents for, and played until it skipped, and which album's score she would memorize in its entirety [which racy-lyric-singing-along-to is curiously never questioned at Charlotte Anne's house]). Rachel Richmond has a boyfriend. Ricky Hernandez, who played the Scarecrow, has been going out with Rachel since the beginning of the year, except for the week when she "quit" him after he came to school with a hickey he'd gotten from Yolanda Jones (Wicked Witch of the West, or "Wicked Witch of the West Side," Rachel called her). Charlotte Anne has no interest in ever being the recipient of a mouth-shaped bruise on her neck and is sure that if any such thing somehow occurred without her consent, she wouldn't go around showing it to everyone like the boys always did. Nevertheless, in the event of a possible hickey, fifth-grader Charlotte Anne Byers wants to be prepared.

One day after school, Rachel Richmond organizes a game of Spin-the-Bottle in the playground, participants being mostly *Wizard of Oz* cast members, including herself, Ricky Hernandez, Charlotte Anne, Sue Ellen Smiley (Glinda), Paul Schwartz (the Wizard), and three boys from the fourth grade who played monkeys. Rachel gets the group to form a circle, puts a Coke bottle in the center of the circle, and proceeds to explain the simple rules of the game, that when it's your turn, you spin the bottle until it points to someone of the opposite sex, and then you kiss that person. (No instructions are provided on the kissing itself, which Charlotte Anne feels might be useful, from the looks of things.) Charlotte Anne, witnessing the hideously moist displays of nine- and ten-year-old kissing, is, during the first few turns, both hoping the bottle will not spin her way and considering her options in the event that it does. For sure she knows she is not going to kiss Rachel's boyfriend, even though he's the cutest boy by a wide margin, and the sight of Paul Schwartz and Sue Ellen Smiley's tongues will figure in considerably to her desire to put this event off indefinitely. What eventually happens is that when it's her turn to spin, the bottle points toward one of the monkeys, all of whom are interchangeably monkey-looking in her mind (not to mention that she's several inches taller than the tallest boy in her own grade, and the tallest monkey is about a foot shorter than she is), and Charlotte Anne takes a good long look at the monkey in question and runs all the way home.

Miraculously, due to her association with the increasingly popular Rachel Richmond, the Spin-the-Bottle incident does little to damage Charlotte Anne's social standing, and she and Rachel start having regular playdates, often at Rachel's house on 85th and Riverside, which Charlotte Anne thinks is the coolest imaginable place to live ever. Rachel Richmond and her brother have their own penthouse apartment. Her mother and stepfather live directly across the hall, and a babysitter lives with Rachel and her younger brother, Kenny, but the kids' apartment is separate and distinct from the parents' apartment, with its very own front door. (The kids' bathroom is in the hall in between the two apartments, but Charlotte Anne sees this as a minor inconvenience, given the overall incredible greatness of their having their very own apartment, plus there are no other apartments on the top floor but there's a beaded curtain at the top of the stairs anyway.) Most super fantastic of all to Charlotte Anne is the decor. Everything in the apartment is red, white, or blue, and there are three tiny bedrooms and a closet along one wall of the apartment, on which wall and continuing across all the doors is a wide red, white, and blue stripe that bends around the corner when it meets the wall, continuing almost all the way to the end of the next wall, where it ends in a giant arrow. (Across the hall, Rachel's mother and stepfather's apartment is done in a similarly mod scheme, in black, white, and silver, with foil wallpaper, black lacquer shelves, and other items like a white leather chair in the shape of a hand [which Charlotte Anne admires but doesn't ever want to sit in as it seems too weirdly literal, like she might just as well be sitting on someone's real hand].) The kitchenette, always stocked with plenty of Tab and a full bowl of M&M's, has a counter with three chrome-and-vinyl bar stools that swivel, one each in red, white, and blue, which makes Charlotte Anne feel very grown-up when drinking the Tab out of a tall glass with a straw. Rachel sometimes tries to make a game out of the kitchenette by pretending they're in a bar, smoking pretzel rods, but the only guy who's ever at the bar is Kenny, who has a habit of spitting pretzel crumbs when he pretends to exhale, and enjoys tossing their Pekingese up in the air like a football, which Charlotte Anne thinks is neither funny nor attractive.

Rachel Richmond also has a lot of Barbies, most of whom, to

Charlotte Anne's surprise, still have their original hair. "Boys like long hair," she says. At Rachel's house, an afternoon of Barbies is a little different. Rachel Richmond's Barbies have sex. Usually, after a brief courtship with a Ken (something like "Hey Ken, what's up? Wanna come over?"), Rachel's Barbie will start mashing on top of the Ken, most of the time with her clothes still on, screaming, "Oh Ken oh Ken oh Ken oh Ken," at which point she usually tries to get Charlotte Anne to be the Ken and say, "Oh Barbie oh Barbie oh Barbie oh Barbie," but Charlotte Anne, who understands that it's good to have a Ken, doesn't much like to be the Ken in this particular Barbie game. (At her own house, Charlotte Anne's Barbie needs are satisfied by a Barbie and Ken fashion show, in which Barbie is heavily featured in a variety of evening wear hand sewn by Charlotte Anne's mom. Charlotte Anne has only one Barbie and one Ken, who has only two outfits, a tuxedo and a pair of flesh-tone ultrasuede pants with a matching fringed vest, so most of the time Ken and Barbie appear in the grand finale in their tuxedo and wedding gown, to an audience of no one.) Plus today, Rachel Richmond puts a Barbie book in the seat of her Barbie's pants, with no commentary until Charlotte Anne, usually shy when it comes to asking questions about things she finds peculiar, dares to ask why she doesn't just put the book in the Barbie book bag. "She's not *carrying* it there," Rachel says, as though this is the stupidest question ever asked. "It's for when her stepfather beats her with a belt." Naturally, this is the first time Charlotte Anne has ever heard of anyone beating anyone with a belt (within the Barbie world or outside of it), let alone preventive belt-beating measures, and although she is aware that she will soon have a stepfather of her own, C.A. harbors no concerns about possible belt-beating, as a trust was established early on when her soon-to-be stepfather bought her a pair of Click-Clacks (two glass balls, in this case a deep blue, joined together by a string you hold on to in the middle, allowing you to "clack" them together, quickly banned from the market in their original form due to a number of incidents in which the glass shattered and literally poked some people's eyes out [there being absolutely no subliminal concerns on Charlotte Anne's part that she was in any danger with the almost-stepfather, or existing mother for that matter, due to their not immediately taking away the Click-Clacks] and lending a renewed credibility to mothers everywhere in the habit of using that phrase), creating a noise Charlotte Anne's mother found rather annoying (which in fact *was* rather annoying, even to her almost-stepfather, except for the almost-stepfather also thought that Charlotte Anne's mom was especially cute when annoyed, and so Charlotte Anne and her stepfather giggled about it together, sealing the bond), solid evidence, she felt, of his overall cool greatness and exempting him from any concerns she might have about the situation. There is no doubt in Charlotte Anne's mind that this is an out-of-the-ordinary Barbie game, even though she never did forget her friend Meg Davidson telling her about the weird penis incident over at Karen Pink-Park's house (the incident, not the penis, being the weird part, as it belonged to their friend Karen Pink-Park's father and was reportedly presented to Meg Davidson as some kind of offering, which she sensibly declined). Charlotte Anne is needless to say more than a little disappointed and disturbed that such mod parents would do such a thing to a ten-year-old girl. Rachel chooses this moment to turn around and lift up her shirt, revealing some decidedly belt-shaped marks across her back. "There's not always time," Rachel says, with absolutely no hint of sadness. "Do you ever think about what it would be like to live in Hollywood?"

"Not really. Do you?"

"No," Rachel says casually, "I just wondered if you did."

Charlotte Anne, adding everything up in her head (belt-beating + Hollywood + ten years old = not good), is entirely alarmed, but taking her cue from Rachel says, "How about if we go fill up the pool?" as eager to change the subject as she is to get out of Ken detail.

Charlotte Anne and Rachel go out to the terrace (actually an unfettered black tar roof partially shaded by a large water tower) to fill up the plastic baby pool, which they're admittedly past the age for, but they figure they can cool off and splash around for a laugh. During a break for Tabs while the hose is filling up the pool, Charlotte Anne gets caught up in a news story the babysitter is watching (about a woman on the Lower East Side who had been brutally murdered in her apartment, and as the story unfolded, it turned out that some ridiculous number of neighbors, like seventeen or twenty-five, had heard her screaming for help, except none of them did, help, and so she pretty much bled to death in her stairwell waiting for help), Rachel goes to lengths to stop Kenny from throwing the Pekingese off the balcony entirely, and the pool is quickly forgotten about until Rachel's stepfather comes across the hall a half hour later, rushing out to the terrace to turn off the water, shouting that the people downstairs are having a flood, that they should have asked permission to fill up the pool, and that Charlotte Anne is to go home immediately. Charlotte Anne leaves, knowing that this is one of those times when Rachel Richmond is not going to have time to go get a book, wishing she'd agreed to be the Ken after all.

A Vast Triangulation

THE FIRST TIME Charlotte met Nicole's new boy-friend she'd heard so much about, she wasn't awfully impressed. Over at Nicole's, after polite introductions to Charlotte and her friend Jenna, Jeff the boyfriend picked up where he left off with regard to the outcome of a Scrabble game they'd just finished and how Nicole could have done better. A sideways glance to the score pad revealed to Charlotte that Jeff had won by a wide margin, and it seemed glaringly obvious that he was simultaneously not men-tioning any possible score-improving to Nicole's friend Chloë, whose score was significantly lower than Nicole's (the implica-tions not seeming to disturb Chloë in any way). Charlotte had never been a big Chloë fan, so she wasn't entirely surprised by Chloë's low Scrabble score or her apparent lack of concern about it, and she was admittedly kind of judgmental. So when the word *nondescript* came into her mind with regard to Jeff, she didn't give it undue attention, knowing that her first impressions were often more harsh than necessary, and also since he'd come with the advance high praise from Nicole. Scrabble weirdness aside, his looks didn't make an impression on her one way or the other, and so at first glance, Charlotte naturally considered the possibility that Jeff and Nicole were representing the standard man-dates-woman-for-sexy-hot-looks/woman-dates-man-for-sexy-hot-mind situation, except for in this particular instance, Nicole was also in possession of a sexy-hot-Ivy-educated mind contained within her sexy-hot body. Charlotte knew rules like these expanded and contracted regularly, as well as reversing entirely (although she never had encountered even one female from the supposedly popular bigger-is-better faction), and that reasonable people of both sexes found a broad range of combinations of personal qualities and physical attributes attractive. At that moment, those were pretty much passing thoughts anyway.

Several moments after the introduction, during which Charlotte took notes on his nondescription, Jeff, who seemed not at all bothered by the current male-to-female ratio (1:4), remarked humorously on a common physical attribute of his present company, specifically their hair, collectively that they had much of it and that he seemed to be pleased with the variety of color and texture represented. It isn't that it was the funniest thing Charlotte had ever heard in her life, so much as it was the sincere way in which it was said, and in the briefest of moments, Jeff's desirability became instantly and deeply apparent, to the point where it seemed preposterous that only moments earlier she had thought of him as nondescript. Charlotte further assessed his good character on several accounts; pulling out chairs, the way he looked adoringly at Nicole, not merely saying *God bless you* when anyone sneezed but articulating each word distinctly and with meaning, taking care to look at the sneezing person directly, in the eye, upon offering the blessing. Also, Charlotte could generally tell the assholes from the nice guys instantaneously (although the presence of this ability hadn't exactly stopped her from dating them); standard asshole behavior almost always makes itself immediately apparent (the broad range of such behavior being too vast to itemize), and Jeff was not presently exhibiting any of those behaviors. Over time, Charlotte had begun to see that some of the ones who had a number of good qualities also had some qualities that mitigated their goodness, not enough to call them assholes, but to effect the need for some new classification that allows for a broad range of personality traits not limited to decent or asshole, but representing the entire range in between decent and asshole. Charlotte felt that there might be room for a modification of terms, such as *semi-decent* or *mild asshole*, thus, in theory, removing the stigma of the asshole name. Nicole's new boyfriend Jeff was a good deal better than nondescript, seemed to be on the decent end of the curve, and for sure he was funny and smart, Charlotte noted, defying any particular asshole categorization, and then the whole group of them stopped hanging out for a while, for no particular reason.

Some time later Nicole got a job out of town and Charlotte and Jeff somehow ended up hanging out kind of extensively. For a while there had been a poker thing going on within the Jeff/Nicole crowd, which included Jeff's friend Al, who ended up having to go to Gamblers Anonymous, and after that it was sort of hard for the rest of the poker people not to notice that they were also getting a little out of control with all the poker-playing. Charlotte was pretty glad she came in on the end of that anyway, because the one time she was about to play, she had a full house in her first hand, and Al said, *Do you know what you've got?* to which Charlotte responded kind of defensively, because she did know what she had but also she was suddenly having flashbacks to when she used to play poker with her stepfather when she was ten or eleven and was the absolute worst kind of loser, stomping out of rooms and making the whole thing worse for herself, naturally, because the stomping and such just made her family laugh, which would make her stomp even more, but inside her head. And so Charlotte was perfectly glad that the poker period had ended before she had any need to join Gamblers Anonymous, except for it was replaced with Scrabble, which, while it had never inspired in her quite such an extreme stomping mentality, did end up being a kind of high stakes sort of thing, even though they didn't play for money. And so the first time she and Jenna were invited over to play Scrabble with Jeff and Al, Charlotte found out that Jeff had this whole policy about games, wherein he felt that games were an allegory for life, and that everyone ought to not only play to win but should also do their best to form intelligent words using as many letters as possible on each play. Charlotte thought that not only was Jeff confusing the meaning of allegory and metaphor, but when you have, let's say, HMQJECP on your little tile holder, it's not worth taking three hours per turn, not to mention that they weren't playing in Czechoslovakian. Al and Jeff were both putting down words like QUORUM and still complaining that they didn't use their extra letter while they were getting like fifty points, or making ZIGGURAT (and of course she had no idea what ZIGGURAT or QUORUM even meant) out of her RAT on a triple-word score and thus getting about a hundred and four points or something.

Charlotte, with her HMQJECP, considered her options and decided the best she could do on her turn was to use her H and M to make HIM, for six points, whereupon Jeff tried to explain that she could have at least made HUM, for eight, at which point Charlotte was like, *It's a game*, and of course Jeff tried to explain further that that wasn't how he saw it. Al, who had never met Jenna before, was trying to restrain himself from an inclination to expand on the Scrabble life allegory, because he thought Jenna was unbelievably cute, even though he was happily married and also believed very strongly in a punishing god. So instead he said to Jenna, *Do you ever see Dilbert?* To which Jenna replied, *Who?* and Al said, *Dilbert, in the paper, the funnies, you know, he works in a cubicle, there's a little cat that makes fun of him — Jeff, where's the paper, where's Dilbert, I gotta show this to Jenna, god forgive me, I have a beautiful wife, but you're a beautiful girl, woman, Jenna, how come I never met you before?* Jenna kind of giggled, and after a while Charlotte noticed that the score was something like 350 to 120 to 46 to 34, and suggested that maybe she and Jenna could forfeit and they could all just order a pizza instead. Jeff put forward the beginning of an argument about finishing things, and how it was part of the whole allegorical game-playing thing, and Charlotte just kind of looked at him like he ought to get a grip, but in a cute way, and he said, *I can't resist that,* and they ordered the pizza.

Al, who didn't know Jenna all that well, said, *Jenna, what are your likes and dislikes? Coke or Pepsi?* And Jenna said, *I like Coke,* and Jeff said very excitedly, *Sugared Coke?* appreciative that a woman in our culture might possibly not drink diet soda, and Jenna laughed, and Jeff called over to Al, on the phone, to order a couple of Cokes, and then Jeff asked her if she preferred letters or numbers, and again Jenna said, *What?* which by now ought to be indicating that Jenna, who isn't stupid, nevertheless sometimes misses some of the subtle humor and/or passion for Dilbert/numbers/letters kind of thing when it comes up in conversation. Charlotte made note of Jeff's effort to include Jenna in the conversation as being another character asset, and also noticed that one of his socks was more of an ankle sleeve than anything, with about one stitch holding together the part that covers the foot to the part that covers the ankle, and she said, *I like letters,* getting back to the original question, and Jeff looked at her like she was the cutest thing ever, but still explained why he preferred numbers, and which ones exactly, and they ended up agreeing at least that 18 is a very good number, being made up of two nines, and also that B is one of the better letters, not just because it's heard as a full word with several different meanings but because it has a good solid sound. It seems safe to say that at that point the mutual-admiration society was fully formed. Charlotte added to her notes on Jeff's character his sharp and sometimes goofy sense of humor and his keen sense of observation with regard to human nature. She had some concern that he was only hanging around her because he thought she was cute, which she would also be grateful for but is inclined to question, generally, although in this case she also felt that since her cuteness might have been overshadowed by Nicole's gorgeousness, maybe he really did think she was smart, untainted by any cuteness, which was still a little bit of a drag, because of course she wanted him to think she was cute and smart, and this led to a circle of thinking that pretty much led nowhere.

Within the mutual admiring, Jeff and Charlotte spent more time together and she began to take his continuing flattery to be sincere based on his apparent inability to censor himself as indicated by his strong opinions on a variety of matters ranging from how the Simpson trial went hopelessly wrong to board games as life allegory to mediocrity on any front, and especially in any form of art. Certainly Charlotte had some concerns that his sincere-seeming high opinion might be colored by his thinking she was awfully cute. At that point, even though Charlotte had begun to build a certain amount of self-confidence (*begun* being the high-point-value word in this clause), somehow she got into a thing with Jeff where she felt a little too worried about what he thought about almost everything, which was probably a pattern she had in relationships even though she was aware that she wasn't even in one in this case, and also that more and more it became kind of a thing where she was aware that she was asking him a lot of questions, not advice so much as what were his experiences with different things that came up, like jealousy, or self-confidence issues, which mutated into a how-do-you-live kind of thing, and Charlotte wasn't exactly looking for a guru or anything, nor did he seem to want that job, but she was interested in his outlook and was also sort of indirectly trying to find out whether his interest in her was strictly platonic or if maybe it wasn't.

In spite of the fully formed mutual-admiration society, nothing happened, because Charlotte, who would go out with some manner of asshole, would not do anything with someone else's boyfriend under any circumstances, and it's not like she hadn't tried to come up with some circumstance under which it would be morally acceptable to her to become involved with Jeff. Charlotte is the sort of person who's inclined to feel guilty imagining so much as a kiss between her and someone who's already involved, the sort of person who can't really even manage a fantasy about a movie star who might be married, much as she finds, let's say, Andy Garcia to be worth imagining, Charlotte is the sort of person who will have to get Andy Garcia divorced, within the fantasy but having nothing to do with having met her, he has to be divorced prior to having met her in order for her to think about kissing him, and so Charlotte tends to find it easier to just fantasize about celebrities she knows are single than to go to all that trouble. It has nothing to do with anything that Charlotte was not at that time in the orbit of any famous people, because for whatever reason it was actually much easier for her to imagine that she would be in their orbit than it was for her to imagine them divorced. Plus, Charlotte knew absolutely that Jeff was still madly in love with Nicole, remember who wouldn't be, and at that point Charlotte believed that Jeff, regardless of any Scrabble-oriented eccentricities, was of impenetrable moral fiber and would never ever stray from his woman, even in the face of some other more true and passionate love, in which case he would surely say only, *No, Helen Mirren, even though I could love you as no man has ever loved a woman before, I cannot leave my woman for you because that is not the right thing to do.* So Charlotte, who wasn't doing very well at all in her efforts to put it out of her mind, tried instead to dismiss the flirtation as not being in any way harmful to anyone and especially since Jeff was obviously madly in love with his girlfriend and also why would he leave Nicole for someone who wasn't even Helen Mirren.

Nicole came back to town for the holidays and confided in Charlotte that she'd had a fling with this guy Charlotte thought of as being something worse than a sycophant and who was also in no danger of getting advanced degrees of any kind. Charlotte was sworn to secrecy before she had a chance to say maybe she'd like not to have known anything about it in the first place, seeing as how this wasn't even the first such troublesome confidence Nicole had placed in Charlotte, and Nicole seemed to feel unburdened somehow for having talked about it, even though the full weight of the burden was felt by Charlotte, who felt somewhat complicitous just for having the knowledge, which she didn't feel quite so guilty about having before Jeff was determined to be a real person. And then Jeff and Nicole started hanging out more, since they were still a couple, and Jeff and Charlotte started hanging out less, and eventually Nicole left town again but by that time none of them were hanging out so much anymore, again, and Charlotte was kind of glad not to have to be acting like she didn't have the awful secret or the crush, which was easier for her to forget when she wasn't having to see so much of Jeff.

Months later, by chance Charlotte ran into Jeff at the Sock Drawer, one of those specialty stores that sells only socks or sock-related items, where needless to say she'd hardly have expected to run into him (seeing as how Jeff had previously seemed to be in no rush to replenish his sock wardrobe and/or organize his tattered socks) and because of that didn't recognize him, even though he will later claim he was shouting her name at the time. Not insignificantly, however, she did notice him, because she did at least see that he was looking at her like, I wonder when you're going to get around to noticing that I'm shouting your name. Furthermore, and more importantly, the other reason she noticed him was because she thought he was really cute, still completely not knowing that she actually knew him pretty well, and for at least as long as it took her to think this thought, which was totally based on what he looked like for this brief moment (which had not been her initial thought about him when she *really* didn't know him), he carried on looking at her until the recognition was made. So they started hanging out again, and it's not irrelevant that Nicole was out of town again, not irrelevant to Charlotte, and as it will turn out, not to Jeff either, but not for the same reason. Charlotte and Jeff picked up where they'd left off with the mutual admiring, but it still seemed fairly harmless because of the circumstances, because of all the already enumerated moral concerns and also equally because she wasn't really interested in getting hurt herself any more than she was in hurting anyone else, and the likelihood in a preexisting-relationship situation in which a breakup takes place, it seemed to Charlotte that more or less everyone gets hurt in one way or another. For her part, Charlotte felt that the total hurt amassed in her series of one-on-one relationships might be equal to any hurt that would come up in a single triangle, and also she had been making efforts to make better choices, romantically, and you know, there wasn't much doubt that someone else's boyfriend wasn't a good bet, even if she could possibly construct some justification on account of betrayal.

One night Jeff invited Charlotte over and Chloë's name came up, and at first Charlotte didn't really notice that it came up in a way that was maybe meant to be casual but was somewhat noticeable because it came up relatively out of the blue, even though Charlotte did at some early point forget who brought Chloë's name up, although she was pretty sure she'd have had no reason to. Which out-of-the-blue conversation seemed to call for some discussion of whether or not Chloë, a painter, was talented, which Charlotte believed strongly that she was not. *Really why do you say that*, Jeff asked, in what Charlotte did not recognize as a concerted effort to sound casual. To which Charlotte rolled her eyes and said, *Uch, I know I don't know all that much about art but that whole thing with the gum wrappers* (referring to Chloë's implementation of gum wrappers and candy products in most of her work, which was drawing some bit of notice in the art world), and then never really finished the sentence except to shake her head ruefully, as if to indicate, *If that's art, there's maybe a slow period in the art world right now or something*. (Charlotte is the sort of person who does go to a museum or a gallery from time to time, and has her own taste, for sure, but not an art-educated one or anything, and even in the face of gum wrapper–oriented art, when she hears people saying things like *The novel is dead, painting is dead*, she just wonders who's deciding all of this, and what isn't dead, although she has a feeling that maybe a blob of jujubes isn't helping to bring it back to life.) And Jeff said, again in a sort of overly casual tone, but also seeming to indicate that he knew more or less that Charlotte was right, *So you don't think she's very good,* and Charlotte shook her head and Jeff quickly mentioned some other artist to make it seem like they were really just talking about art in a general way, and muttered some theories about the art being tied up with the person. *Meaning what, exactly,* Charlotte asked, knowing pretty well that Jeff's idea was that if a person was bad at their art that their depth as a person was probably limited. Which he did say, in his own construction of words, to which Charlotte said, *And what about their* goodness *as a person,* because you can be sure by then that Charlotte was feeling that they were talking about more than just art, that the Scrabble mind-set figured in there somehow with regard to her, that they were not talking about Chloë at all, that Jeff probably thought it was Charlotte who was not very deep, and could care less about her goodness as a person. And so when he said, *Charlotte,* with his most sober face (which tended to precede his turning around to his most sincere and charming face as a manner of teasing), *I think you're the cutest thing ever,* Charlotte decided she really didn't know what to think about any of it.

It's possible that a big long talk with Jenna confused the issue some. For obvious reasons, Charlotte tried to relay her quandary in the abstract. Jenna, who does have a clear sense of right and wrong when she actually knows what someone is talking about and who had no idea that the core of the issue was about whether or not Charlotte should go ahead and move in on Jeff (which Charlotte of course knew she should not but was looking for some, any small justification), interpreted the entire story as being hypothetical and launched into a long discourse about the need to live honestly, how important it was that people express their feelings and how sad it was that fear so often kept us from living our dreams and especially how it kept us from really connecting with people. Charlotte's deep-rooted concern about not living as honestly and fearlessly as she could long predated her association with Jeff, and of course at that time, she was indeed not living honestly — if she were, she wouldn't have been sitting around having a deep conversation about it with Jenna. There would have been some honest and fearless activity occurring in place of the deep conversation about honest and fearless living preempting the need for naming it as such, ideally, with Jeff.

The next day, Charlotte decided she would tell Jeff the truth, more or less, and she actually did call him up to say, *If the circumstances were different I'd be all over you in a heartbeat,* and possibly because of it being a phone call it was somewhat less courageous than if she'd marched over to his house and pushed him down on the couch or something, but still she was trying to be honest and fearless but retain some kind of propriety (even though she didn't really know what she'd do if he suggested they did get involved, which she was nearly certain by then that he wouldn't, which possibly made the whole situation safer than any kind of results of honest and fearless living she had been hoping for would have been, except for the honesty part), and he reciprocated the sentiment even though she didn't totally hear him to remember his exact words because she was kind of too nervous to hear.

The day after that, undoubtedly under the duress of some of their recent conversations, Jeff revealed, under an oath of secrecy (having given her word, Charlotte will keep all these oaths even if it means she might go a little silently mental), that he had indeed already strayed, and to make matters worse, with Chloë, about whom Charlotte has had not entirely unwarranted ill feelings, not at all because of her questionable talent but because Chloë once went to a party at Charlotte's house and then the next day or maybe a week later acted as though they'd never met, and it wasn't like it was some big party where maybe you might not have ever had a chance to meet the host, this was a party of maybe eight. Not to mention in Charlotte's modest apartment it would have been pretty hard not to notice exactly who was there. Meanwhile, Chloë, Charlotte knew, was unavailable to Jeff in a thousand ways, even though that didn't stop him from thinking he was in love with her, and that somehow he would overcome the obstacles of his having a girlfriend and all of the reasons why Chloë was unavailable as well as her being a bad artist, which was the most difficult of all things he needed to reconcile for himself, which Charlotte naturally thought was a little bit misguided. Worst of all to Charlotte was that there turned out to be some element of retribution in Jeff's having gotten involved with Chloë, not lessening the actuality of his or her feelings necessarily, but being a considered factor on the part of Jeff, who insisted that his lust for retribution was entirely new to him, which Charlotte decided to believe, because she still dug him, even after all this information came out. Jeff explained at length to Charlotte the whole thing he had worked out in his head about *do unto others,* which he interpreted vehemently as some kind of nearly literal eye-for-an-eye deal, some kind of situation where, Charlotte guessed, if someone kicks your dog, you kick their dog, putting aside the poor innocent dog, and how therefore his involvement with Chloë was totally justified, seeing as how Nicole had slept with the guy Jeff knew about the whole time. Charlotte, who recognized in Jeff her own need for an editor in any number of areas in her life (ranging from things people usually use editors for to needing someone to come over and say, *You could maybe stand to throw out, let's say, your checks from ten years ago,* or in Jeff's case, his allegories and his sock wardrobe), cut him off and tried to point out that maybe the meaning had gotten lost a little, that as she understood it it's not about keeping score but that it's essentially about karma, and that the end of the quote was not *what they actually do to you,* which seemed to be the idea Jeff had worked out in his head, but something Charlotte knew was more like *as you would have them do unto you.* If he was going to live by the philosophy he'd worked out, she explained, *If it's about math,* then he was, as it happened, not even, because there had been three dalliances on the part of his girlfriend that they both knew about, two existing prior to the sycophantic guy, not one, and it certainly would have served Charlotte if Jeff chose to recognize and act upon this. She suspected he wouldn't, of course, because then he'd absolutely have to admit how very off this sort of idea was to begin with, and also, she'd have to live with it too, which she wouldn't care to, seeing as how it would go from being some attempt at honest and passionate living to some kind of scorekeeping situation, and of course Jeff would still have to go sleep with someone else besides Charlotte in the interest of catching up. In which case Charlotte would have moved from the already difficult original (albeit only imaginary) romantic triangle consisting of points J, N, and C into intersections of geometric shapes she had no interest in knowing about.

Nicole came back and it was pretty obvious that she knew Jeff and Charlotte had this mutual crush, the worst part of the whole thing being that she enthusiastically reported, *I'm so psyched you and Jeff have been hanging out, that's all I hear now, Charlotte this and Charlotte that,* very exclamation pointly and clearly indicating a total lack of concern that Charlotte and Jeff were ever going to engage in anything more than flirting, which she appeared to be aware of and entirely unworried about. Jeff broke out the Scrabble, but early in the game when Nicole added the letters TRIANGU onto Charlotte's LATE, Jeff said in an unmistakably condescending tone, *Just because you heard it on the news doesn't mean it's a word,* to which Nicole tried to explain what it meant. To which Jeff said, *I know what it means,* without any indication that his sense of humor was still available to him. Nicole flipped through the dictionary and read, *Triangulate, verb. One. To divide into triangles. Two . . .* Charlotte felt the beginning of a stomachache and decided to go home, after which no one called to ask her how she was feeling, after which she thought there might be some entirely new permutations of the asshole category, and they all stopped hanging out again.

✦

A Malicious Use
of the List Format

✦

CHARLOTTE ANNE BYERS makes the transition from public to private school with relative ease, but the bump up from sixth grade to seventh proves more difficult. A recent fifth-grade graduate from P.S. 166, Charlotte Anne had looked forward to enrolling at I.S. 44 middle school with then–best friend Rachel Richmond (who would run away from home before the end of eighth grade anyway after a particularly brutal belt-beating from her stepfather), but on a tour of the school with her mother, new stepfather, and other visiting parents, rumors of stabbings and children flying out of windows went around and it was decided that Charlotte Anne would attend private school. Initially, in spite of the rumored stabbings, after five years in public school, Charlotte Anne has strong reservations about private school that focus largely on uniforms. In fact, the only dress code at Davis Academy is no clogs or sneakers, which doesn't sit well with her either but is a more tolerable concession than a short plaid skirt (she had given up skirts and dresses entirely as of the end of third grade and at the urging of Rachel Richmond made a foray into hot pants that lasted exactly one day). Charlotte Anne, somewhat shy, survives an interview with the surprisingly genial headmaster, who, impressed by her almost entirely "excellent" elementary-school grades (non-numerical grades ranged from poor to excellent, hers marred only by consistent "poors" in penmanship), as well as her perfect attendance record, admits her to the sixth-grade class.

Challenges at Davis Academy, of an entirely different origin than those at P.S. 166, call for adjustments. Although she considers herself a pacifist, Charlotte Anne has become accustomed to the ever-present possibility of having to beat someone up. (She's never actually seen or even heard about an actual beating-up incident, but there were always threats, and one had to assume, however Midwestern and unthreatening one appeared, a badass posture, one Charlotte Anne would never entirely shake. Plus there was that one time in fifth grade when defenseless Sue Ellen Smiley supposedly both talked smack *and* snapped on Yolanda Jones, a dubious allegation at best, since S.E.S. retained her southern manners throughout her five years at P.S. 166, nevertheless Yolanda attempted to orchestrate a group beating-up after school, threatening to additionally beat anyone up who didn't take her side and getting several of the fifth-grade girls, including Charlotte Anne, to agree to participate on the beat-up-or-be-beaten-up basis, the beating-up of Sue Ellen Smiley quickly aborted when their homeroom teacher discovered the plan, much to Charlotte Anne's combined embarrassment and relief, having no beating-up skills and considerably less interest.) At eleven, her concerns are intellectual. Charlotte Anne Byers has a class called Current Events. A weekly project is to take a front-page article from the *New York Times*, paste it into a scrapbook, and be prepared to discuss it in front of the class. The predominating news stories of the time are Vietnam and Watergate, and Charlotte Anne Byers is both years away from an interest in politics and developing a considerable fear of public speaking/raising her hand (a time will come in the future, long after most hand-raising opportunities have passed, when she'll have trouble not speaking publicly, even without being asked, but at present, being called on is becoming an issue). Additionally, students are encouraged to mail away for a P.O.W. bracelet for ten dollars, the significance of which is unclear to Charlotte Anne except that the popular kids all have them and most everyone else, including her, doesn't. Her mother and stepfather, not of a liberal bent, having unwittingly provided their daughter with a decidedly left-wing education (which will, at a total cost of more than $14,000, transform said daughter into a confirmed liberal before she graduates high school), will not exacerbate the damage by sub-sidizing the bracelet based on a show of solidarity for the war victims ("Sweetheart, that ain't gonna bring them back," her step-father said) nor on the "everyone has one" argument (at no time in the history of her youth did this argument ever end in favorable results), finally forcing Charlotte Anne to stash three weeks' allowance in order to mail away for the bracelet herself, which would end up turning her wrist green in a matter of hours.

Charlotte Anne survives her first year at private school by being pulled into a small group of friends vaguely proud to not be the most popular. Clarisse Benjamin sits next to Charlotte Anne in the back row and bonds with her during a class trip to the Metropolitan Museum of Art when they discover they both love *From the Mixed-Up Files of Mrs. Basil E. Frankweiler* and think it would be fantastic to stow away like Claudia and her little brother, funded by coins from the fountain. (Charlotte Anne hasn't yet been to Clarisse's house and wouldn't know that her own romantic notion of sleeping in Marie Antoinette's lounge chair and enjoying the riches of the fountain wasn't so much a dramatic improvement in lifestyle for Clarisse as it was motivated by the desire for a place of her own without any parents pretending they actually lived there too.) In addition to the *New York Times*, this year has the sixth graders reading Kurt Vonnegut's *Cat's Cradle*, a considerable literary leap up from the previous year, and which mostly befuddles Charlotte Anne except for the amusing use of language. Having no idea what it's actually about (she will read it again twenty-five years later and still not know), she and Clarisse Benjamin think *Cat's Cradle* is the funniest book ever, which results in the girls forming their own religion, the prime tenets of which involve the wearing of a certain type of loafer and that their disciples curtsy before them and refer to them as "O Great [Whoever]" (that no one ever joins is not in any way bothersome to either Clarisse or Charlotte Anne). An after-school study date at Clarisse's Park Avenue apartment makes an indelible impression on Charlotte Anne, with six bedrooms, marble floors, two kitchens (one with a dumbwaiter), four bathrooms, a live-in maid, and a pantry stocked with every conceivable type of snack food available. She is most impressed by two things, though:

1. Clarisse has her own bathroom that has a chrome toilet-paper dispenser operated by a push button that springs the door open, revealing the toilet paper (which Charlotte

Anne did not previously understand to be so unsightly as to require a hidden dispenser).

2. Clarisse's mother and father have separate bathrooms on either side of their bedroom, and her mother has a dressing "suite" that includes two walk-in closets, one just for shoes.

Charlotte Anne lives with her mother and stepfather in a prewar "two-bedroom" (Charlotte Anne's bedroom technically being the dining room, which is a source of torment for her during dinner parties, on which occasions C.A. gets the boot from her own room, and also because of its location between her parents' room and the kitchen, severely limiting her privacy; her mom will say, "Knock knock," and then walk through without waiting for an answer, and it should be noted that there is an alternate route to the kitchen via the front hall that adds maybe an additional five seconds to the trip that Charlotte Anne's mother is rarely willing to take), and their entire apartment could probably fit into Clarisse's parents' bedroom suite, the apartment not made any more comfortable for three people by a single bathroom (there is a toilet in a dark closet off the kitchen, but a scratchy toilet seat and a claustrophobic feeling keep all of them away unless absolutely desperate). During their study date (mostly Charlotte Anne is studying Clarisse's lifestyle), the girls discover another common interest: making lists. After making the list of rules for their religion, Charlotte Anne and Clarisse make a list of things they have in common:

1. making lists
2. like actor Wally Cox (who they know only from his appearances on Hollywood Squares)
3. like the word *humble*
4. same shoes
5. address begins with five
6. blue eyes
7. been to Rome
8. prefer fountain pens
9. founders of the Divine Order of Blue Loafers

Then a list of things they don't have in common:

1. Clarisse's parents are married
2. Clarisse has a brother
3. Charlotte Anne has been only at the Bangkok airport, Clarisse has seen the actual city
4. Charlotte Anne has read *The Harrad Experiment* (Charlotte Anne's mother has an inexplicable habit of giving her daughter her books when she's done with them, regardless of subject matter. By the time she's twelve, Charlotte Anne will have read *Portnoy's Complaint*, everything by Jacqueline Susann, *Fear of Flying*, and those sex books by "M" and "J," as well as regularly taking the quizzes in *Cosmopolitan* [on which her scores were generally off-the-chart low for obvious reasons]; several years later she'll wonder if this was her mother's way of avoiding "the talk," which seems unlikely given that her mother and stepfather talk about their own sex life quite a bit

more than any twelve-year-old would care for, and which dinner conversation/possible sex education is not enhanced at all by literature using terminology such as *probe* or various words related to the presence of a high temperature)

5. Clarisse prefers neither Keith nor Danny Partridge but rather Reuben Kincaid (a peculiar choice even for an adult, as well as an ill omen)

Charlotte Anne openly questions the existence of Clarisse's parents, as she has never actually seen them; Clarisse claims they do in fact exist, but although there is evidence of some upper-class life form, Charlotte Anne has seen only photos. Clarisse hosts a sixth-grade graduation party while her parents are in Morocco; nearly the entire class attends and participates in a kissing game called Teacher Teacher in which it's theoretically better to fail (depending on who's failing you) because you have to continue kissing your "teacher" until you pass. Despite a lack of parental supervision, this party is inexplicably attended by the two sixth-grade teachers (not in the game), Mr. Grady and Mr. Josephs, who seem entirely neutral about the goings-on. Charlotte Anne and Clarisse, along with classmate Leslie Bacon, decline to participate (this is Charlotte Anne's second experience with kissing games and it doesn't look any more enticing to her this time with the addition of several mouths full of braces), and Jenna Ritter declines the invitation altogether with a note saying, "No, thank you," which Clarisse felt was sarcastic and joked that if Jenna couldn't play Teacher Teacher with the actual teacher then she wasn't going to play at all (which was an unfortunate reversal of what was probably true; Mr. Josephs had on numerous occasions made it known to the entire sixth grade that he thought Jenna was the prettiest girl in the class, which, in addition to being completely creepy, was occasionally rumored to be the reason for Jenna's extended absence).

The summer after sixth grade, Charlotte Anne goes to Iowa to visit her actual dad and Clarisse goes across the country on a teen tour (not yet twelve, Clarisse is a full two years younger than anyone else on the tour). Charlotte Anne gets several letters from Clarisse in which her adventures escalate from seeing Wally Cox's handprints at Grauman's Chinese Theater (photo enclosed) to dropping acid with a ninth grader from Tenafly named Judd. Equally as appalling to Charlotte Anne as the acid-dropping is Judd from Tenafly. Apparently he cuts class.

Though Clarisse makes early efforts to continue the friendship upon her return in the fall, Charlotte Anne is unable to reconcile Clarisse's increasingly troublesome behavior; by the end of the year she will be addicted to marijuana (Charlotte Anne does not bother to investigate the actual addictive quality of marijuana, being satisfied that seventh graders who smoke pot every day, go to class stoned, or don't go to class at all have a pretty bad problem) and have a twenty-four-year-old boyfriend (refer back to list #2, item 5) with whom she has regular intercourse in the back of his head shop (twelve-year-old Charlotte Anne has been in quite a number of newsstands offering paraphernalia unrecognizable to her but has just come to learn the term *head shop*). Clarisse drifts away from Charlotte Anne and toward Leslie Bacon, an almost-member of the D.O.B.L. (mutually rejected upon the basis of her loafers, which, while identical in style, were brown) who has similar proclivities and double-dates with the twenty-four-year-old's twenty-three-year-old business partner. (Though twelve-year-old Clarisse, like Charlotte Anne, is already 5'6", C.A. wonders where exactly they go on their double dates that no one bothers to say, "Um, excuse me, Mr. Cool Ponytail Guy, shouldn't you be *in jail?*")

Overheard by Peter Schneck, Charlotte Anne's horror, expressed solely and quietly to classmate Jenna Ritter by the fourth-floor lockers, gets back to Clarisse, albeit in a somewhat altered form ("Clarisse is on drugs and doing it with some old guy" being translated to "Charlotte told Jenna that you were a pot-smoking slut"), and the following day a slip of notebook paper falls out of Charlotte Anne's locker with the following list:

Reasons I Don't Want to Be Friends with You
1. you're uptight you should try pot it might help
2. you're jealous you should try sex it might help
3. bitch

Charlotte Anne, devastated by the loss of the friendship as well as the malicious use of the list format, slowly relents to the friendly advances of Jenna Ritter (which friendship will endure, to their continual astonishment, through disco, new wave, grunge, and the boy bands [which Jenna loves unashamedly], as well as a troubled marriage, a variety of losses, and a few time zones), with whom she also has things in common:

1. like French
2. embroidered overalls

3. live on Upper West Side (though this will be the cause of some debate between them; Jenna pretty much feels that if it's north of her, it's more or less the Bronx, while Charlotte Anne feels certain that her apartment on 89th and West End is both a recognized part of the borough of Manhattan and also a part of the Upper West Side)
4. aspiring writers
5. scholarly fathers
6. against pot
7. against sex with old men

Jenna and Charlotte Anne move past their initial reservations about each other (Jenna will spend the early part of seventh grade thinking C.A. likes Clarisse better because C.A. once said she wished she were Clarisse [which memory bank of Jenna's will figure into their relationship in future decades, when Jenna will recall many things once said by Charlotte Anne that Charlotte Anne will not only not remember but not think anymore, like let's say that she wants to marry Parker Stevenson], which was mostly just because of the toilet-paper dispenser, but she doesn't; Charlotte Anne has early concerns about Jenna's mental health involving her mysterious absence in sixth grade, initially explained by a diagnosis of mono, which everyone figured maybe wasn't the only reason after a few months went by, and Charlotte Anne still doesn't know why Jenna was absent all that time but doesn't feel compelled to ask), and Jenna's availability/not-sleeping-with-old-men quality makes her an increasingly desirable best school friend (eventually bumped up to best all-around friend).

Jesse Jackson,
He Lives in Chicago

I.

It is not an admission too many daughters want to make.

One brief look in the mirror confirms the obvious.

Charlotte is exactly like her mother.

Okay, maybe *exactly* is an exaggeration. In fact, what it is is that she is 50 percent like her mother and 50 percent like her father, which is a totally weird split if you know the two. It is at best a good balance and at worst something of a psychosis. These are not personalities that willingly share space.

Which would explain the divorce. Which would explain a lot of things.

It becomes impossible to ignore when her mother suddenly decides to move to Arizona. That this imminent move coincides with Charlotte's need for cash is not good for either of them in many ways. They meet for sushi on 81st and Broadway. Her mom orders a cup of miso soup and a bowl of edamame.

That's all you're eating? Charlotte says.

I'm not hungry.

Her mother has recently lost some weight.

Mom.

Edamame is very good for you. It's soybeans. I'm not hungry, leave me alone.

Your pants are hanging off you.

I've been working out.

Mom.

I can't breathe here anymore. This city is suffocating me. Your father doesn't understand me.

You mean my stepfather.

You know what I mean. No one understands me. I need to go.

Go?

I have to get out of New York.

This much, from where Charlotte is sitting, is understandable. Charlotte has been trying to get out of New York for years. It's not nearly as simple as booking a one-way flight. People get drawn back. Places seem inferior. Which fact, coupled with an inability to function well in the place where you're from, the place where everyone but you wants to be, can lead to anguish, confusion, immobility, and/or a tendency to leave and come back repeatedly, alcohol and drug abuse, and sometimes a mental state equivalent to having a cheerleader and an incubus inside your head, debating.

Go where?

Arizona.

To see Aunt Bonnie?

I'll stay with Bonnie and then find a place.

You're moving there?

I can't live here anymore.

Her mother's fingernails are bitten down as far as they can be bitten. Farther. The thumbnail on her left hand is nearly gone.

She's got a Band-Aid on it, but Charlotte knows what's under-neath. Nothing.

Mom, why do you do that? she asks as her mother gnaws at her remaining thumbnail.

Without taking it out of her mouth, her mom says, *I can't help it.* And then she cackles. Her mom has a master's degree in social work.

Stop it, Charlotte says, pushing her mother's hand away from her mouth.

It's your stepfather's fault.

Stop it.

I'm serious. I wouldn't be under this kind of stress if he listened to me. He doesn't think the way I do. He doesn't care about psychology. He says, "Get over it." I can't get over it.

Get over what?

Never mind. He doesn't understand.

What doesn't he understand? He loves you. To say that her stepfather loves her mother is an understatement of epic proportions. Her stepfather thinks her mother is the most beautiful, most brilliant, funniest thing ever. And she is rather obviously beautiful, with crazy thick dark hair and green eyes, and she's tall, with enviable super-straight posture. She's not someone you miss when she walks in the room. Her stepfather's devotion to Charlotte's mother is displayed partly in the way he looks at her after all these years and partly in the way he laughs too loud when she says something funny even though mostly what she says that's funny isn't meant to be funny, for example she likes to tell jokes except she can't ever really remember them, and she'll say something like,

Oh there's this frog, and he's in a bar, or on a bar, and he says to the bartender, "Bartender" — *something about peanuts* — *oh wait, I think there was a what-doyoucall, a rabbi or a priest,* and then she cracks up, and she kind of does this when she tells stories too, and you know she knows what she's trying to say, but you have to kind of help her fill in the blanks, sometimes, or put the story in the right order, which is not to say that she is stupid in any way, because she isn't, and which is more a sort of charming characteristic than a humor-oriented characteristic, and which arguably does have its appeal. But they do fight. About money, and trash removal, and fast driving.

I'm just tired.

Mom, just go to a spa.

I'm not spending two thousand dollars to go to a spa for three days to come back and undo two massages or some herbal seaweed whateveryoucall bullshit — facial wrap in an afternoon at Fairway with the shoving and the bus fumes all over the pears and beans. I need to leave.

At this point, it has become clear that there is not going to be any good time to mention the need for money, especially not money to go to Los Angeles. Ten years earlier Charlotte had moved to L.A. with everything but her mattress, on the heels of the fourth breakup with her then-boyfriend/boss from the pizza place (and subsequent ill-timed reappearance of same boyfriend immediately after the purchase of the ticket but prior to the leaving of town), with some idea that she was going to meet with superstardom, except the superstardom plan wasn't completely thought through. For one thing, she hadn't exactly chosen a field; although she has since childhood imagined picking up her Oscar, the category has never been determined. There was some thought that by the time she grew up they would give out Oscars for Best Novel (and that by then she would have written one), or that maybe she would just get some kind of honorary Oscar for her distinctive life observations made in everyday conversation, or the occasional letter. She had taken a few acting lessons after a creepy director suggested she had "a quality." But eleven days of living in a leaky Laurel Canyon house with no TV proved to be her mental equivalent of Chinese water torture, and she flew right back. It has never been more clear to her than at this moment that she is so not adopted.

Mom, I need to borrow a little money.

This is not a good time. Why. You already owe me money. I don't suppose I'll ever see that.

Mom. I'm going to go see if there's any work in L.A. My friend has an extra room I don't even have to pay for right now.

Do I even have to bring up what happened the last time you went to L.A.?

Mom, I'm not going to move, I'm just going to sublet for six months and see what happens. I need to work. I think my friend can get me a job on her series.

How much money?

A thousand?

Charlotte Anne. This is a very bad time for me financially. Your stepfather is going to be very upset. He doesn't even know right now that I'm leaving.

You're telling me first? Mom —

I can't believe we're having this conversation again. He's going to take all my money when he finds out.

No he isn't, Mom. He really isn't. Charlotte's stepfather is not vindictive. He's just not a screwing-over kind of guy.

I need my money to go away with. I don't know what's in my future, career-wise. I'm not twenty-five.

Charlotte will find out later that her mother, at this time, has a total of holdings in the vicinity of a million dollars. Charlotte, who is clearly no financial genius, has a good idea how far she could make a million dollars go even if she never worked another day.

When are you planning to tell him? What about counseling? Something.

No, we've tried that. He goes but he just thinks we need to "move on." He doesn't want to really hear me. I'll tell him as soon as I get everything set up.

Mom, don't ask me to lie to him.

I'm not asking you to lie, I'm asking you not to mention it.

Please tell him soon.

Charlotte's mother writes the check and hands it over. *This is just a loan. I want this money back.*

Okay, Mom. Thanks.

Charlotte's mother pushes away the half-eaten bowl of edamame.

I think I have a little bit of an eating disorder, she confides with her cute-guilty look.

I think so, Mom.

I'll be fine.

2.

Charlotte's mother rents a midsize U-Haul, drives to their country house in Vermont, loads everything she owns into the U-Haul, drives back to the city, loads everything she owns into the U-Haul minus a minimum of home furnishings for her husband, and drives herself to Arizona. Charlotte gets on a $99 Tower Air flight to L.A. with one suitcase and a laptop.

3.

There isn't that much to say about what happens while Charlotte is in Los Angeles, at least not anything that can be said to further illuminate the troublesome single-mindedness of the city of L.A. that would explain why Charlotte's plans are not long-term, but for the purposes of wrapping up: Charlotte exchanges numerous bizarre phone calls with both her stepfather and her mother in which her stepdad speculates that her mother is having an affair in Arizona, in which her mother continues to blame her stepfather, in which Charlotte has flashbacks to inappropriate confidences made twenty-five years earlier about her real father, in which it becomes more and more clear that her mother is not having an affair in Arizona but is rather experiencing whatever kind of low-level breakdown allows a person to still walk around and possibly find employment. Charlotte does get a job on the aforementioned series, buys a thirty-year-old muscle car primarily because it is available and in the price range her father has donated to the cause, drives from Venice to Burbank and back every day, has any number of driving-related freak-outs/auto maintenance–related financial setbacks that will ultimately eat up about everything she earns while she is in Los Angeles, is suddenly very romantic about changes in weather and the noise and crowds of the subway on her drive from Venice to Burbank every day, flies back to New York about every obscure holiday for the duration of the nine months that she is in L.A., except for Thanksgiving, when she goes by way of Chicago to see her dad in Iowa, which if you know even a little about geography you know is about three hundred miles west of Chicago and therefore six hundred miles out of the way. Charlotte had worked on a movie in Chicago as a script supervisor two years earlier and has some unfinished business there, which is mostly that she just likes the place. It seems like a place to live. It seems like a place she might not come back from. It's hard for Charlotte to pinpoint the pull she feels to Chicago considering its obvious similarities to New York, e.g., tall buildings, museums, theater, shopping. She doesn't really even know what the people are like, which is of some concern, because she has a disproportionately large fear of guys who wear baseball hats and read *Stuff* or *Maxim* and have modern apartments with six remotes and possibly an étagère from IKEA and nothing hanging on the walls except for maybe a bike, and she has the same sort of fear of women in cropped khakis and Rachel haircuts who seem healthy and happy, and feels Chicago may have an abundance of these healthy and happy men and women, which is not something she really relates to at this point, the health and happiness, but it's not about that either. And there's a big lake, of course, New York doesn't have a big lake, and it's a very big lake and that counts for a lot, and there are also garage sales, you don't get a lot of garage sales in New York, and there's Casimir Pulaski Day and Sweetest Day, she's not exactly sure what either of these are except for they're two more holidays, and Jesse Jackson, he lives in Chicago, and on Saint Patrick's Day the river is green, you don't have that in New York, but for Charlotte it's not exactly any or even all of these things together. In a way it's not unlike attraction, like why one guy and not another? Charlotte can't really explain it. It's the melancholy feeling she gets watching *ER* and they mention someplace she's been, like the Oak Street Beach, or a café in Wicker Park. In Chicago she stays at a hotel that overlooks the lake and when she looks over the lake she has some deep thoughts about life and god that escape her the next morning and when her credit card won't cover the second night she leaves early for Iowa.

4.

Charlotte's mother calls when she gets back to L.A. She is back in New York.

We bought a house in Jersey, she says.

Who is we? Charlotte asks.

Me and your stepfather, Charlotte.

Oh. Well, great.

He loves me.

I know.

I'm not very good on my own, her mother says quietly.

I'm too good on my own, Charlotte thinks. Charlotte thinks many things at the moment, from relief that this lapse is over, to relief that she will not have to endure either of their separate love lives, to doubt that things will ever be the same, to doubt that things really should be the same, to hope that her mother will be happy in New Jersey, to hope that her mother will be happy some-where, to hope that she will be happy somewhere, to hope that she'll decide on an Oscar category, at the very least.

It isn't discussed again. A year later there is a big twenty-fifth-anniversary party where friends come from all around, where silver gifts are given, where catered food is served, where it is not discussed again.

By then, Charlotte is in Chicago.

5.

One of the many reasons she's never left New York for long is because of the driving thing, which is multilayered in scope and often debilitating. And she does, after she gets back from L.A., have an unprecedented moment in the subway in which her appreciation for New York is accelerated, when, in spite of her ongoing New York–related problems (in no small part a matter of crowd control/personal-space maintenance), she thinks, This is great, the subway, the subway is *cool*, driving is *lame*, the subway is for *real* people. Look at the tile, the tile is so great, there's no tile on the freeway, there's nothing but Fatburgers and short pink buildings and more freeways on the freeway, you're not out among the people on the freeway. It has always seemed to her that the so-called freedom associated with cars heavily promoted in most of the U.S., or, you know, all of the U.S. *but* New York, is a lie, that this ongoing falsehood is perpetuated in, among other things, every car ad ever made (whereby freedom is allegedly flat-out unavailable without car ownership), and that the truth is that to live in a city such as New York where mass transportation is so abundant and where walking, whether as a matter of preference or if need be, is a legitimate means of travel, to be unburdened by car ownership, by auto maintenance and insurance (what is liability anyway, shouldn't it be non-liability?) and titles and payments and traffic and *parking*, to name, seriously, just a few — that, Charlotte thinks, is the real freedom.

This subway-related enthusiasm lasts about a day and ends when someone trying to get off the train gives her a flat tire without apology. There are so many people squashed up next to her that she cannot even bend down to fix the flattened sneaker and spends the next three stops concerned that she will lose the sneaker altogether in the process of getting off the train, which in fact does almost happen. Someone steps on the loosened laces and the shoe *is* almost abandoned in between the train and the platform until it is finally recovered with a lucky jerk, which results in an accidental shove to the girl trying to board the train at the same time, which results in Charlotte yelling at the girl for trying to board the train before everyone else disembarks the train, which results in the girl calling Charlotte "Bee-otch," all of which results in Charlotte remembering what is wrong with the subway and the entire city of New York. Were this just an isolated incident, Charlotte would have no beef, but the memory that such incidents are rather daily, often hourly, in a city where there is no physical room for such incidents not to happen, Charlotte's best solution to this problem, most of the time and unfortunately, is to stay in.

Which brings us to the matter of Charlotte's apartment, which is not the ideal place to stay in for periods of time extending beyond sleep, wardrobe changes, matters of personal hygiene, and the occasional mail check. Which of course is not how much time Charlotte spends there. It's a confusing matter, because again, there is this concept, much like the freedom thing, a New York version of the car/freedom thing, a propaganda, Charlotte feels, whereby if you hold the lease to any apartment of any size at any location in the borough of Manhattan that is under a thousand dollars, you should uphold the following rules/laws/principles/beliefs and/or feelings:

a) under no circumstances shall the Lease Holder (hereafter referred to as LH) relinquish the lease of the apartment, for a period no less than *all of time*

b) LH shall at all times feel privileged to hold said lease, in spite of any evidence to the contrary such as but not limited to: comparable or significantly larger apartments in other cities that rent for some small fraction of what LH's apartment rents for; issues related to building maintenance such as security, plumbing, and any depression apparently resulting from residency in said apartment

c) LH shall brag whenever possible

and

d) should it become necessary for LH to vacate the apartment for any reason such as work, marriage, or other, LH shall sublet said apartment for anywhere upward of double what LH is paying

and maintains the right to

I.) charge an exorbitant "finder's fee"

2.) include requirements in a "sublease" specific to meeting LH's personal needs such as mail-forwarding, plant-watering, ex-boyfriend management, landlord/across-the-hall-neighbor management (supposing that either LH or sub-LH might ever actually run into them), e.g., that you are LH's lesbian lover, dog walker, or personal trainer (applicable where size of apartment warrants).

Should LH at any time be in violation of these rules, he or she shall be considered in noncompliance, shall risk being called crazy, shall risk status as true "New Yorker," and shall relinquish all hope and/or chances of ever finding a deal like this again.

(The word *deal*, Charlotte thinks, being used far too liberally.)

This propaganda, widely held within the confines of New York City and coupled with the whole New York–as-capital-of-the-world thing, is extremely difficult to debate, particularly when one is from this particular place. Because inside of the particular head of Charlotte are certain thoughts that, whether true or unfounded, cause a certain paralysis with regard to ever leaving, putting aside the apartment issue briefly, certain aforementioned and admittedly snobby thoughts about how everyone outside of Manhattan conforms to the khaki and baseball-hat culture, a generic culture where people seem happy with the same rotating-cast romantic comedies, not because they really are but because they think they're supposed to be, how there cannot possibly be book-reading, interesting people she might want to spend any significant amount of time with in any of the outer boroughs much less outside the tristate area, certain thoughts that render her unable to leave the dark, cluttered, $978-a-month, single-3'×2'-closeted, painted-shut-other-window-facing-windowed, walk-like-a-crab-narrow-no-sink-in-the-bathroom, only-sink-in-kitchen, must-brush-teeth-in-kitchen-sink-where-there-are-frequently-still-dishes-present, overpriced-custom-built-floor-to-ceiling-can't-take-it-with-you-shelved studio apartment (so especially wrong for a person who has a habit of never getting rid of anything; Charlotte's read more than one article about some elderly eccentric who collects this or that, sometimes it's news-papers, sometimes it's suitcases or TV sets, so many suitcases or TV sets that they pile up to the ceiling and the elderly eccentric has to move around the apartment through tunnels of suitcases or TV sets until somehow *the authorities* find out about it and declare it a fire hazard and the elderly eccentric has to get rid of most of the suitcases or TV sets but instead of feeling unburdened feels sad and torn about what to let go of, like it's the *Sophie's Choice* of suitcases and TV sets, a scenario Charlotte can easily envision in her own future), which apartment-not-leaving results in more apartment-not-leaving.

6.

Naturally, under these conditions the idea of any kind of employ-ment, relocation, or dating becomes difficult, and so when Char-lotte's friend Jenna proposes that she must come out and meet her friend Todd, she is less than enthusiastic about the proposition for numerous reasons, including:

a) it involves going out
b) it involves going farther than the Korean market up the street
c) she has no money
d) literally no money
e) it sounds like a fix-up, which is something like a date, which is something she is now against, for all the same reasons anyone loses interest in dating, because it is understood that in spite of the potential for brief moments of rapture characteristic of the beginning of such entanglements, it is widely known that such rapture has a way of holding one's normally rational mind hostage long enough to convince them that it will work out, which as far as Charlotte is concerned is a cruel, cruel joke.

Jenna, an especially accommodating friend, a friend who has known Charlotte since junior high, a friend who is as familiar with Charlotte's stubborn nature as with her own powers of persuasion, comes by to pick Charlotte up to find that Charlotte is wearing a large gray sweatshirt seeming to indicate that Charlotte is not yet ready to go. *No, not going,* says Charlotte. Jenna spends some time modifying her description of the occasion to convey its casual, unimportant nature, to convey its utter one-hour-of-your-life essence, to remind her how much she loves the cinnamon-laced decaf at Café Lalo, that from her apartment Café Lalo is equidistant to the Korean deli, that she will spring for both the cinnamon-laced decaf and a slice of Umanoff & Parsons' chocolate mud cake, which she knows is Charlotte's favorite, at which time Charlotte agrees to go partly for the mud cake and partly because Jenna is not leaving her apartment.

Initially, it appears that Charlotte will return to her apartment entirely unaffected by the casual decaf meeting. Todd is not presenting any of the characteristics that usually appeal to her, namely that he has never been, holds no interest in being, nor does he in any way look like an actor. It's not that Charlotte is looking for actors. She just finds them. They are abundant in her business, they are abundant in Alcoholics Anonymous, and they are abundant in the food-service industry. Todd describes himself as a filmmaker. This is probably the only clue to any potential problem, as Charlotte has always had a hard time not hearing that word in italics, that that word often presupposes some kind of art/statement-making, which presupposes pretension, not to mention the internal conflict that arises given that she has filmmaking aspirations of her own but would like to avoid pretension, e.g., she could go the opposite route and say she makes movies, to make the point of being down to earth, but which she worries could portray her as trying to be down to earth but really being just as pretentious as the next guy, which at this point is neither here nor there considering that all Charlotte is really doing about the filmmaking at this point is secretly writing, but to get back to the dating issue, since we know that Charlotte is looking for no one, not actors nor waiters nor filmmakers, the combination of her looking for no one and Todd's not making any kind of initial overwhelming impression on her allows Charlotte to relax and engage in conversation with Todd without concern for the entirety of their future. At some point Charlotte becomes aware that what is happening is not so much conversation as interview, an interview with questions that are not so much questions as they are an interview for a position for which all other applicants are no longer being considered, an interview in which the questions are not so much unusual as they are numerous and exclusive of Jenna, who is sitting right there and is not at all displeased to be excluded, as this may be the first match she has ever made of any success, inasmuch as even one party has interest in the other, which Todd obviously does, although it is hard for anyone to miss the change in the angle of Charlotte's head from interest in Todd as a friend of Jenna's who she will never see again after this mud cake to interest in having another piece of mud cake at which time Jenna will not simply be excluded but will not be present at all. Charlotte herself is not sure how this transformation of Todd has taken place in the course of the eating of the mud cake. She can plainly see that he looks exactly as he did when she walked into Café Lalo, that his hair is still uncombed, that his purple plaid short-sleeve Land's End shirt is still tucked into his slightly too highly hitched jeans (which border perilously on acid-washed), and that his jean jacket is still hanging on the back of his chair, which, when they leave, will turn the aforementioned outfit into what Charlotte considers to be the contemporary version of the leisure suit. Charlotte is sure, faced with denim-on-denim, that she must really be interested in this guy. She is only grateful that it is a little too chilly for sandals.

Charlotte and Todd say goodnight and nice meeting you and they smile that way and before he says goodnight in his denim leisure suit, Todd hands Charlotte his e-mail address on a slightly chocolatey napkin. *I'd love to read some of your stuff.* Charlotte, who has sort of lied in the interview and said that she has no stuff, reiterates that she has no stuff, since it's not stuff she's ready to show anyone at this point, to which Todd says, *Well send me an e-mail anyway.* Todd walks away, Charlotte looks at the chocolatey napkin and then at Jenna and says, *Fuck. This is going to make it very hard to leave town.*

7.

In the end, the opposite will be true, and there will be other things that make it hard to leave town, but in the meantime, right about here there could very well be another lengthy insane boyfriend story. There was a lengthy insane boyfriend story here in which Charlotte, under the duress of wanting to leave town but not knowing how, started by accepting Todd's invitation, on the first date, to get into a very small, very old stick-shift car that she was barely able to drive, for a cross-country road trip in which he more or less psychoanalyzed her, and her mother, and his mother, and anyone who's ever had a mother, been a mother, knows how to spell *mother*, or has anything to do with motherhood in any remote way, from coast to coast. To say much more seems needless except insofar as it leads to the part about her getting out of town. They did have a few good minutes early on at Joshua Tree, in spite of Todd's idea that they should ingest mushrooms for a spiritual experience. Charlotte tried to explain to him the many ways she thought *spiritual* and *mushrooms* did not belong in the same sentence, and also that in the program you don't get to do drugs of any kind. His mother had been sober for some time, you'd think he'd have known this, plus he's not stupid, nevertheless he tried to debate Charlotte on account of her not having done massive amounts of drugs and because her primary substance of choice to abuse had been alcohol. Somehow they got past this and had a decent time at Joshua Tree. You're not supposed to camp there without a permit but they did anyway, setting up a little camp underneath some kind of rock formation, and they hiked a little and Charlotte barely slept because there are no lights and she could see the stars in a way she'd never seen them before, like if there had been time she could have counted every one, and also had as close to a spiritual experience as she's ever had, minus mushrooms, wherein it suddenly seemed a revelation to her that the earth rotated, because she'd look at the moon and it was there, and then it was there, and then it was there, like in those stop-motion movies where it's speeded up and it goes *shoop* across the sky in about five seconds. Her mistake was getting back into the car after the sun came up, knowing she should have said, *You know, this is as good as it's going to get, I'll just catch the bus.* Anyway, you could just as well insert your own insane boyfriend story here, everyone has at least one or twenty, although you might want to ramp it up about fifteen times, and title it *How to Leave Town the Hard Way*, and you could have him be the typical arty/angsty guy who "isn't about" any or all of the following:

things
success

money
bringing babies into a precarious world
time
electricity
the phone
insert your own basic human twentieth-century desire or need
    (maybe your guy isn't about food, or breathing)

(and who will, not very long at all after this lengthy I.B.S., appear
to be very much about all of the things on this list and more insofar as he marries rich and brings babies into the precarious world)
but who is about, who seems currently to exist only for and be
solely about metaphors as his own unique means of psychoanalyz-
ing you.

    Todd is, granted, one of the more extreme examples of mental
unrest that Charlotte has come across, and there are some really
good examples of things he says that are so unbelievable that you
might like to know about them anyway. Like the thing about
metaphors. Like everything is a metaphor for something else, like
nothing really is what it is in and of itself, e.g., on the second day
of their road trip, their rearview mirror breaks and Charlotte has
the idea of getting it fixed while Todd has the idea that it's a
metaphor because Charlotte, metaphorically, doesn't need to see
behind her, but rather to look ahead. Or she's blue because she
wears so much blue. Also he thinks people who have too much
actual stuff have too much emotional stuff, which sort of pushes
Charlotte's buttons because she does have way too much stuff and
would like to get rid of some of it, but not all of it, like Todd,

who goes out of his way to rid himself of his own actual stuff so that some minor illusion is created that his emotional stuff is also worked out, to the point where he doesn't have like, a chair, which is pretty obviously something most people need, one chair, and then he'll try to say he's not about that, and Charlotte will say, *Chairs? You're not about chairs?* and it becomes a crazy exercise in craziness, but by the time this is discovered, Charlotte has already been sucked into the vacuum because you have to admit it's fascinating even if it's ultimately exhausting, and it will cause her to reexamine some of her own worldview, which he will take credit for, except it won't be in the way that he thinks.

8.

A recap of the real reasons Charlotte is blue at this time:

1) Charlotte is broke
2) Charlotte is unemployed
3) Charlotte is on a road trip with someone inclined to use words like *bardo*
4) Charlotte's mother has just been diagnosed with cancer.

9.

There could be another lengthy cancer story here. You could likely insert your own lengthy cancer story here and call it *How to Do All the Wrong Things When Your Mother/Father/Sister/Best Friend Gets Sick* and you could include any or all of the following.

Feelings of:

> extreme and overt hostility toward the ailing relative/friend
>> (in Charlotte's case it starts with being pissed off at her mother going and getting cancer when she's trying to leave town)
>
> flashbacks/reliving entire confusing childhood
>> (ranging from average daily weirdnesses like why Charlotte had to eat store-brand cornflakes with powdered milk for breakfast when her mother got to eat leftover Entenmann's banana cake to why her mother didn't encourage her more to be a singer, or a filmmaker, or whatever she wanted to be, considering)

Details about:

> paleness/helplessness/hair loss
>> (like the time Charlotte's mother tried to break away from a lifetime of hot rollers by using a round brush and a blow-dryer and got the brush stuck in her hair and Charlotte had to work it out and her mother put her head in her hands, which by the way, with only marginal aging and advanced-stage nail-biting, looked identical to Charlotte's, and her mother said, *I'm going to lose my hair* and tried to make it look like she wasn't about to cry.

Mom, you're not going to have chemo. It's not the cancer that makes it fall out.

I know but I don't want to lose my hair.

You're not going to lose your hair.

I don't want to lose my hair, she said again, smoothing it down.

Mom, you're not making any sense. You can't lose your hair.

Gillian from next door's daughter lost her hair. It never came back.

Mom, she had alopecia.

That's a stress thing, you know, I have stress.

You're not going to get alopecia.

Well, I have to be careful about that.)

and/or

    surgical scars/depression of ailing relative/friend

        (like the long crooked one down Charlotte's mother's back; *Look, Charlotte, I'm bionic,* she said, or the way she kept the curtains closed most of the day even though no one could see in and there was lots of sunshine over her garden otherwise, except it was almost like she didn't want to know about it if she couldn't fully participate in it, she was never a halfway-participatory kind of gal)

Duration and quality of:

    crying/attempts to avoid this in presence of ailing relative/friend

        (assume that in this case all of the above were numerous, phlegmy, sometimes loud, often leading to breathing problems and the need to excuse oneself from the room)

Reconciliation and/or profound gratitude for ailing relative/friend:

        (e.g., the broken hammer Charlotte's mom got at a garage sale for fifty cents after Charlotte's flew out the window, or handmade doll clothes, or handmade Charlotte clothes, or the birthday cake for her ninth birthday with roses all the way around so everyone got one even though it cost a lot extra that she didn't really have, or for the best stocking stuffers, or the Spanish Steps, the Coliseum, and the Catacombs, for letting Charlotte sit at the cappuccino bar by herself at age eleven in Milan, for taking her at age ten to see *West Side Story* and *Wuthering Heights* in Tokyo [w/Japanese subtitles], for taking her on the bullet train to see Mount Fuji, going shopping in the Zona Rosa in Mexico City, for not letting Charlotte drink the water in Mexico City, for taking Charlotte up the ski lift in Aspen, in spite of her fear of heights, for taking Charlotte horseback riding in the mountains in Aspen, in spite of her fear of heights, for skiing in Vermont [see: aforementioned fear of heights], for going up Pikes Peak [see: skiing in Vt., ski lifts in Aspen], and crossing the world's highest suspension bridge at Royal Gorge [see: Pikes Peak], for getting Charlotte a Shih Tzu, for a complete and total lack of grief about the kinds of things kids generally get grief about, e.g., staying out late, [not] getting straight As, messy rooms, going to see the musical *Hair* for Rachel Richmond's tenth birthday party, buying Charlotte the record and subsequently not flinching when it finally occurred to Charlotte to ask what *cunnilingus* was, for reupholstering Charlotte's queen-size sleeper sofa with white fabric even though *it's so impractical,* for knitting an afghan for the reupholstered sleeper sofa, for never throwing anything away that Charlotte might possibly have wanted or needed, for teaching Charlotte to sew, for teaching her how to make a quilt [and telling Charlotte it didn't have to be perfect because none of hers were, even though careful examination of the evidence proved otherwise], for ripping apart everything Charlotte sewed that came out bad and putting it back together [which might seem like a mixed message except for when you put two sleeves on the right side of a dress and someone fixes it, it's just better], for making Charlotte a Cowardly Lion costume for *The Wizard of Oz*, for *The Bad Child's Book of Beasts*, *When We Were Very Young* [her copy], and *Harold and the Purple Crayon* [her copy, tragically lost], for approximately fifty blank books [no longer blank], for reading *Little Women* to Charlotte out loud every night for a week in fourth grade after Charlotte forgot she had a book report due, for taking her to Bil Baird puppet shows, movies at Radio City Music Hall, the Metropolitan Museum of Art, the Museum of Modern Art, for taking her ice-skating at Rockefeller Center, roller-skating in Vermont, out for lobster in Maine, to see Old Faithful and *The Nutcracker*, and for never even suggesting that they see *Cats*, for Davis Academy, for always telling Charlotte she's beautiful, for undue forgiveness Charlotte had not always extended to her)

and, if relative eventually dies,
Details of freaky last moments such as:

just happening to be in town when it happens

how it happened right after a holiday or your birthday and
how it seems like they "waited" for you to get there
dog appearing to look sad when you come back without
deceased relative/friend
sense of god and/or deceased relative/friend being present
such as curtains suddenly blowing even though the window's closed, hearing something come out of your own
mouth that deceased relative/friend might say

And then some more about:

the duration and quality of the crying and possibly creating a
little museum/shrine in your house to them and then scal-
ing back a little later when it seems a little morbid and then
a lot of missing the person all the time and/or forever.

The character details will always be different, but the rest has only
so many variables and in this case begins with Charlotte wondering why this is happening to her, with Charlotte realizing kind of
late in the game that the cancer part of the story is not in fact
happening to her, with Charlotte remembering kind of a lot of
good things about her mom (see gratitude list above) and that the
reason she hadn't encouraged her to be a singer or a filmmaker or
whatever she wanted to be was because she had struggled so much
herself, and because her success didn't fix her like she thought it
would, and because she wanted something easier for Charlotte.
Which ends with Charlotte realizing her mom did the best she
could with the information available to her at the time (more or

less one copy each of Dr. Spock and *I'm OK — You're OK*) and making efforts to appreciate her mom while she's still around. Which gets back to Todd insofar as he somehow is able to convince her that she doesn't have to have a job, or an apartment, or a friend even, anything that seems like a reason that most people might move somewhere, that she should trust her feeling and just go, even though he'd really rather see her move to someplace that doesn't have electricity. At this moment Charlotte wishes more than anything that she could just float right out of Todd's bitter little universe into someplace where things don't hurt with such a spectacular constancy, and after her mom is pronounced cancer-free (another story entirely because although there are a few decent years where this seems true, it will later be clear that the cancer was not free but in captivity at an unknown location), Charlotte decides to just go. The bonus here is that her mom is pretty cool about it now, because she knows that detours out of town, lengthy cancer stories, lengthy insane boyfriend stories, and crazy road trips sometimes add up to something, even if it's as simple as knowing when to come home and in Charlotte's case realizing that she could actually live someplace where she had to drive, someplace that might be home, someplace like let's just say Chicago, which has been haunting her like an old boyfriend ever since she left.

✦
Notre Monde
✦

THE GIRLS MEET in seventh-grade French. Technically, they've already met, the year before when they were both
new, but they were in different homerooms and Jenna was absent a
lot, prompting much gossip and speculation about mono. So it
might be more accurate to say that the girls are thrown together in
seventh-grade French, where Charlotte Anne is doing marginally
better than Jenna (the fact is, it's the beginning of the year and
she's coasting on a stellar accent), and Madame Goldstein suggests they study together after school.

Jenna Ritter doesn't know what to think about C.A. Byers and
is mostly concerned that this need for academic help will only
serve to elongate the shadow cast by her older brother, Eric, des-
tined to discover a miracle cure for like, everything.

Charlotte Anne thinks this is a really, really bad idea.

Charlotte Anne is not a big fan of Jenna Ritter.

Charlotte Anne thinks Jenna Ritter doesn't *have it together*.

Charlotte Anne Byers, age twelve, has a big thing about *having it
together*. (Charlotte Anne's mother does a lot of talking about
people having it together, and how great it is that her daughter has
it together since she says *please* and *thank you* and doesn't do drugs,

which is all well and good, except for that a) there's plenty of time and b) this doesn't account for all the other ways one might not have it together, especially when they sort of appear to have it together on the outside but on the inside seriously don't, or are perhaps currently establishing the foundations for how they will not have it together in the future.) Lots of kids in their grade don't have it together at all, mostly in the form of them smoking pot in Central Park after school (a social group identified as "parkies") and having sex with whoever, which Charlotte Anne thinks is both disgusting and indicative of severe mental troubles. Charlotte Anne's assessment of Jenna's severe mental troubles is based not on drug use but on her mysterious sixth-grade absence (which C.A. does not attribute to mono at all but speculates that Jenna *just didn't feel like it*, which gets off onto another tangent because sixth was Charlotte Anne's first year in private school, and she'd come into the school with some very fixed ideas about snobbery, namely that rich kids, which she was not, kind of get to do what they want, which includes not going to school if they just don't feel like it, which in Jenna's case was not in fact what was going on, even though Charlotte Anne was sort of on the right track at least insofar as Jenna was probably mildly depressed). This plus Jenna's habit of wearing the same outfit (a long-sleeve maroon Lacoste shirt and a knitted cap) pretty much every day causes Charlotte Anne to diagnose Jenna with an advanced type of hang-up that she doesn't think she wants to know more about. An argument could be made that Jenna is still at the fashion advantage, as Charlotte Anne, who wears different clothes every day, is not wearing anything especially cool, which equals any of the following:

a) anything as nondescript as Jenna's outfit (more passable than cool, since her Lacoste shirt is regarded as sort of a classic, and therefore neutral, although Charlotte Anne is not the only one who notices that Jenna repeats)

b) a tight, ideally pale blue t-shirt with rhinestones on it that spell out something like HOLLYWOOD or FOXY

c) a t-shirt (any color) bearing the Pandemonium Boutique logo of a giant Charlie Chaplin head

d) a worn-in college t-shirt, any color, preferably from an Ivy League

e) kneesocks, with everything

and

f) Cork-Ease (pron. *corkies*) "Buffalo" sandals, in tan (thick suede cork-soled wedgies with straps that crisscross in the front).

Charlotte Anne Byers does not have any of these things. In Charlotte Anne's heavy rotation right now are:

a) a pair of overalls with a bunch of tiny ceramic pins on the front (a duck, a heart, a paintbrush, and a Coke bottle) and a cluster of diaper pins hanging from the hammer loop (mysteriously, a trend)

b) a longish gingham smock top with patch-front pockets that her mother made

c) a pair of newfangled blue-and-tan saddle shoes with "marshmallow" soles (these go with everything)

d) anklets, also with everything

and

e) in cold weather, a jacket Jenna likes to call Charlotte Anne's "Big China Coat," a quilted parka with a Chinese pattern and bamboo buttons that Charlotte Anne thinks is the greatest thing ever, if admittedly on the puffy side.

Choice *a* doesn't usually bring her too much grief. Choice *b* regularly results in her being teased for looking like she's wearing a maternity outfit. Choice *c* she seems to sort of get away with, because saddle shoes are actually in style (fifties nostalgia, due to *American Graffiti* and *Happy Days*, is in full force), but part of the problem with regard to the saddle shoes, and a general problem Charlotte Anne suffers from fashion-wise (besides essentially being at the mercy of her mother, who will *certainly not* buy her daughter something *just because the other kids are wearing it*), is that she wants both to fit in and also to have her own style, and so she will occasionally, and in the event that her mother agrees, purchase the cool item, but in a different color, which is nearly always a mistake, socially, not to mention that she's not really a big fan of sandals anyway, and so with regard to the purchase of the navy suede Cork-Ease, although there will be some grief at home about the sandals after they are later found under a pile of dust bunnies at the back of Charlotte Anne's closet, this ends up being one less front on which she's abused at school, since the sandals give her terrible blisters on her heels. Kneesocks have never been an option. Charlotte Anne has thick calves. Not a good look with the thick calves, since they only come three-quarters of the way up and generally don't stay up anyway. Which is unfortunate, because anklets, it is widely known, are for babies. (Which of course creates some irony as far as the whole diaper-pin thing is concerned.)

So it should be clear that Charlotte Anne and Jenna are not exactly in "the group" ("the group" being so cool that a single article suffices as modification where some less cool group might apply an adjective). It's a small school, and an arty one, so things could be worse, and there is a tier below them that is steadfastly uncool, comprised of the super-bright kids and the thoroughly misfit kids. But they're at a critical juncture here. Charlotte Anne's friends from sixth grade got into partying over the summer, which poses a major problem for her having-it-together lifestyle. Jenna used to have one friend from her building but no other close friends from sixth grade, except maybe her sixth-grade teacher, who openly proclaimed her the prettiest girl in the grade, which Charlotte Anne finds both creepy and a moral outrage (Charlotte Anne loves to talk about morals, which she feels there is a severe lack of), but which she also bitterly and secretly resents since it's not her. Both girls, in spite of their present state of moderate uncoolness, are actually very pretty — Charlotte Anne, with an all-American blue eyes/light hair/freckles combo, and Jenna, a more exotic, dark-hair/dark-skinned beauty with a killer smile —

but have such a lack of style that for the time being it goes unrec-
ognized. Charlotte Anne, it might be useful to know, is mystified
by the fact that she is not considered pretty at school, because
she's been walking around since forever thinking she was pretty
much Miss Thing; she was a beautiful child and almost did some
modeling (which idea went astray, as Charlotte Anne was a somewhat sullen little girl and therefore lacked the requisite perkiness
needed to sell anything), and no doubt because of her mother's
daily reminders (fueled by her not having gotten any such
reminders when she was a kid) still feels confident about her
looks, to the point where she thinks that any kids unable to recognize this are just wrong. Jenna, on the other hand, is subject to
day-to-day changes insofar as her confidence is concerned, which
by and large is dependent on her not feeling fat, or on some rare
occasion, one of the popular girls saying she's cute when she takes
off her hat. Most of seventh grade is a wash for Jenna feeling very
good about her looks due to her having cut her hair very short in
an effort to look like her mother. Most of the seventh-grade girls
have not yet advanced their hairstyle beyond long and parted in
the middle (the coolest), long and parted on the side (acceptable),
or the occasional and somewhat bold "China Chop," a bangs-and-
chin-length style that involves a newly popular appliance, the
blow-dryer, but which isn't terribly flattering even on the cutest
girls and takes more time than is currently cool. Charlotte Anne
has actually gotten her very long, side-parted (Mom's insistence)
hair cut just before school started (at Vidal Sassoon, for a splurge)
up to her shoulders, which is acceptable, if a bit triangular, which

will be a lifelong problem as Charlotte Anne has naturally thick hair, which, when shorter, leans to the triangular shape.

And what does Jenna Ritter think? Jenna Ritter thinks mostly nice things. Jenna Ritter has neither a good nor a bad opinion of Charlotte Anne Byers at this point, which makes it all that much harder for Charlotte Anne to be irritated by Jenna, even though C.A. is irritated by many things at the age of twelve, not just the boys who are eight inches shorter than her and say her smock top looks like maternity wear, not just by issues of moral outrage, but also seventh-grade math, and anything that generally strikes her as "dumb," which is a lot of things.

So Jenna calls Charlotte Anne to invite her over for a French "date" (why there is never any confusion or abuse, in seventh grade, about the use of this term for an entirely platonic, girl/girl occasion, remains a mystery), in which phone call Jenna will later claim Charlotte Anne was severely unfriendly, mostly by way of a lot of impatient huffing, and a date is arranged for the following afternoon at Jenna's apartment in the Dakota. Part of Charlotte Anne's huffing is on account of Jenna insisting they live in different neighborhoods; although they do live eighteen blocks apart, it's still walking distance, and Charlotte Anne says everyone knows that it's all the Upper West Side, and interprets possible snootiness due to Jenna's Central Park West address (despite Jenna's assertion that her address is actually on 72nd Street), same neighborhood or not, being considerably fancier than West End Avenue, where Charlotte Anne lives. In fact, there is no snootiness; if anything it's Jenna's own attempt to be different, but not necessarily better — Charlotte Anne and Jenna will later agree, snootiness or not, that the West Side, overall, is better than the East Side, overall (except for the unjust location of Bloomingdale's), due to a severe snootiness level present on the wealthier East Side. (Which, of course, is true, and in this case, as a matter of coincidence only, fits their paradigm.) The reality is that Jenna's (artist) mom and (author/publisher) dad could afford to live on the East Side and just don't. Charlotte Anne's (opera-singing) mother and (talent-agent) stepfather could maybe afford to bump up to Riverside Drive, but that's about it. Private school, at a little more than $2,000 a year, was given quite a bit of consideration, and chosen as much for the education value as because the public middle school in Charlotte Anne's neighborhood was seeing an upsurge of kids throwing other kids out windows, which swung the decision to drop the cash on the side of safety. In any case, Jenna, at her age, is showing no signs of a certain quality present in most city kids by the time they hit third grade, rich or poor, which is a sort of calculated indifference, no doubt due to having witnessed murders and child killers and muggings, even if only on the news. Charlotte Anne has already witnessed more than a few of these things not on the news and, as a news junkie from about the age of ten, finds it impossible to believe, when the subject later comes up, that Jenna has not, at the very least, seen an exposed penis at some point in her existence. (Jenna will be a little defensive on this front, since she has in younger years seen both of her brothers naked, but Charlotte Anne insists it's only the unwanted, grown-up penis exposure she's talking about.) Charlotte Anne saw her first from inside a subway car at age seven; a stereotypically trench-coated older guy, in between cars, flashed anyone in sight, explained by her mom as an example of someone way past not having it together and firmly in full-on perverted. Charlotte Anne finds it impossible to believe that Jenna thinks New York is "beautiful," and although Jenna will cite Central Park, Rockefeller Center, and the Empire State Building as examples that Charlotte Anne will neither deny nor confirm (annoyed at the possibility that New York might be more than one thing), when she asks Jenna, "Haven't you ever even run into Ugly George?" Jenna will say it's not nice to call someone ugly even though Ugly George is a self-monikered cable-access host who roams the streets half dressed in search of young women interested in undressing themselves for the camera. (Not so much a precursor to *Girls Gone Wild* as a poorly lit perversion unto itself.) This is the era of garbage strikes and a Times Square inhabited by prostitutes and drug dealers and a vague specter of that soldier kissing the nurse after the war, with the dimming fluorescence of the Bond's sign and the giant smoking billboard; even traveling from Charlotte Anne's house into Jenna's own "neighborhood" requires traversing Amsterdam and then Columbus Avenues, which are notoriously crime ridden and generally Charles Bronson–movie-inspiring scary, populated with men whose eyes linger on Charlotte Anne's developing form and offer various unsavory invitations or yell, "*Mira, mira,*" which Charlotte Anne learned from Ricky Hernandez back in public school means "Look, look," but which translation unfortunately came after she had already looked at a few more parts and gestures than she cared to, eventually teaching her to travel most regions of the West Side with eyes narrowed and fixed ahead as though no one exists in her periphery at all. (Charlotte Anne's mother has some reservations of her own about her daughter going over to Jenna's, but it's less about the dangerous travel than that she just saw *Rosemary's Baby* on the *4:30 Movie*, fortunately C.A., even at twelve, has the good sense to point out to her mother that Satan probably doesn't really live there, to which she will say, "Well, it's still spooky.") On occasions when they convene at Charlotte Anne's, Jenna will typically get a ride in her dad's Cadillac or take a taxi down 72nd and up West End Avenue, thus bypassing any less beautiful parts of the neighborhood and arguably eliminating them from the landscape altogether. These divergent perspectives will change very little over the following thirty years, even as the broadly defined U.W.S. neighborhood (ultimately extending up as far as and perhaps even beyond the limits of Columbia) gains an entirely new reputation as a hub for urbans of a young and professional kind and changes almost entirely into a neighborhood that one does not have to be afraid of except in a Pottery Barn kind of way.

A few minutes into their date, Charlotte Anne is already frustrated by Jenna's absence of any sort of edge, and yet, a few minutes after that, will be charmed as most are, given the opportunity, by Jenna's unrelenting niceness (even in the face of Charlotte Anne's overt ho-hum attitude), her sense of humor/ability to laugh at herself, and ironically, the very unironic overall quality Charlotte Anne claims to detest. Going into the friendship, there are certain unknowns of a similar nature that for better and worse will help forge a bond/dependence between them that will take a lot of therapy and twelve-step work to remodel twenty and then some years into the future. It turns out that Jenna's mysterious sixth-grade absence/correctly-diagnosed depression by unlicensed-therapist-in-training Charlotte Anne was due as much as anything to a letter from her former best friend/only real friend (in this case also best building friend) Debbie Alsop, who more or less explained that she had obtained a new best all-around friend and would no longer be needing Jenna's association. Charlotte Anne, who still has a best building friend and a couple of other newish school friends since the move up to seventh, is still smarting from the malicious list from her former best school friend Clarisse calling her a bitch and implying that sex and drugs might be of use. (Charlotte Anne would have a lifelong issue with non-dog-oriented use of this word from this point forward, even in jest. Her general good sense of humor, even about herself, as a rule tends to show no signs of its existence in incidents of name-calling or even when gently teased, say as by her mother and stepfather, who do it kind of a lot.)

The exact amount of seventh-grade French that gets discussed this particular afternoon, or ever, is negligible. They might or might not sit down for a moment and open their copies of *Notre Monde* before some distraction causes them to abandon their textbooks for good. By the end of the year, Jenna's grades will go up and Charlotte Anne's will go down after Mme. Goldstein's discovery that her grammar doesn't come close to matching her accent. In three weeks' time, Charlotte Anne will officially stop "tutoring" Jenna in French and officially become Jenna's best school friend.

Charlotte Anne and Jenna have a lot of after-school dates at both of their houses. Each has reasons for preferring dates at the other's house. Jenna has better food (although the menu Jenna offers tends to be a bowl of Familia cereal, frozen pigs in the blanket, or a jar of green olives), and with the vastly bigger apartment and building, more territory and therefore more variety, even though they quickly settle into the curious routine of an episode of *The New Zoo Revue* (there's no accounting for this; it is a show that is considered weak even by its intended audience of preschoolers), Familia, and a game in which they drop pins down the center of the stairwell, race down the stairs, and see who can find the pin first. This is really what they do. Jenna also seems amused by a game in which they take the elevator to the top floor of her building, where the four sections are connected by a series of narrow and dark corridors of maids' rooms, inhabited by a decidedly creepy element (notably an old guy with a very bad black toupee and thick black spectacles who always seems to be standing on his doormat in a white t-shirt, on the lookout for some unspecified danger), followed by Jenna running away at an undisclosed time and letting Charlotte Anne find her way back. Jenna makes a frequent point of telling Charlotte Anne how much she reminds her of Debbie Alsop, and although Charlotte Anne does not know about the letter, she notes that Jenna makes just as many separate points about how bossy Debbie was, which in Charlotte Anne's mind sort of unconsciously adds up to an insult. The truth is that Jenna envies both Debbie's and Charlotte Anne's apparent strength, independence, and fully formed opinions on just about anything that might come up (a notable development, as there were several years in elementary school in which Charlotte Anne's opinion on just about anything tended to coincide with the opinion of whoever she happened to be talking to; it was never that she didn't have her own, just that she had a fear of saying out loud that let's say she didn't much care for the idea of peanut butter and marshmallows together in a sandwich, for fear of alienating the peanut-butter/marshmallow-eating person; her typical answer to any question that began with "Do you like . . . ?" began with "Do you?" and proceeded from there). Charlotte Anne in turn envies Jenna's apparent rose-colored view of New York, although she'd never admit it, and spends much time trying futilely to explain to Jenna the horrors of the very same.

At Charlotte Anne's, a significantly smaller two-bedroom, activities tend to be limited to watching *Dark Shadows* and the *4:30 Movie* (which everyone knows repeats their four themes about every month, which adds up to Charlotte Anne having seen every Annette Funicello movie ever made, and both *The Bridge on the River Kwai* and *What Ever Happened to Baby Jane?* about a dozen times each), avoiding Charlotte Anne's mom, who refuses to put on pants simply because there's company (and who Jenna seems to like anyway), and possibly making some additions to their *Charlotte Anne Digs the Dorks, Jenna Luvs the Losers Random House Dictionary*, volume II, which contains a combination of current slang terms and words they made up altogether. Charlotte Anne and Jenna are both writers. Jenna is planning to be a playwright. Charlotte Anne wants to make movies.

In April of that year, Jenna invites Charlotte Anne to her family's house on Fire Island for a weekend. Charlotte Anne has heard of

Fire Island but has never been there. Jenna and Charlotte Anne create a new routine, modified from their city routine, wherein their day consists of going to the beach, doing Mad Libs (somewhat less fun for the girls, who fancy themselves of a sophisticated wit, when Jenna's younger brother plays and much like C.A.'s own stepbrothers is inclined to use adjectives and nouns relating mostly to things found in, near, or around the toilet), playing pinball in "town" (neighboring community that has several small shops, bars, and restaurants), and riding bikes (during which Jenna modifies the "lose Charlotte Anne in the building" game to "lose Charlotte Anne on Fire Island" game, by leading Charlotte Anne leisurely through several neighboring communities and then riding away really fast to see if Charlotte Anne will find her way back, which she always does, which always results in Jenna being slightly miffed. Neither of them bothers to think through what might occur if Charlotte Anne really did get lost, but Fire Island is a fairly easy place to get around, being three or four blocks wide in most places and having alphabetically lettered streets. Not to mention that Charlotte Anne is not at all stupid and easily able to navigate the simple courses Jenna has attempted to lose her in. Another thing neither of them is bothering to think through is why Jenna is doing this in the first place — neither is particularly competitive, and Jenna insists she just thinks it's funny. Charlotte Anne isn't morally outraged, probably because she does always find her way back, but neither does she think it's terribly funny, writing off Jenna's lapse in sophisticated humor to her having brothers). One of the best outcomes of the weekend in Fire Island is that they return to school with tans (or in Charlotte

Anne's case, a sunburn and a lot of freckles), which elevates them socially, if only the tiniest notch. Charlotte Anne will spend several more weekends at the Ritters' on Fire Island during the spring and summer, before she leaves for Iowa to see her real dad.

A final opportunity for humiliation is present at the annual Davis Academy event called Moving Up Day, which takes place in the yard near the end of the school year. Although a casual occasion, each grade from one through twelve has a sign that is ceremonially handed off to the grade below, officially marking their entrance into the higher grade. It's a day that might be tolerable if it were left at that, but the other focus is on various school awards in each department for excellence in achievement, and the Jane Berman Award, named for a megastudent of days past, ostensibly awarded to the student who contributes most to their class or to the school in terms of extracurriculars and overall good attitude, is universally (mis)understood to be the popularity award. This year it's Jenna's brother Eric's turn, for having participated in the school paper, the science fair, and the chess club, and also for filling in for the librarian at lunchtime. (There has not been and will not be a year when Eric Ritter doesn't win something, for which Jenna suffers in silence, dreaming of the day she might get the Jane Berman Award.) Charlotte Anne expresses to Jenna her ongoing moral outrage over the school administration's perpetuating such an elitist proposition, excluding those for being shy (Charlotte Anne likes to think of herself as shy but really has more of a very specific attitude problem whereby if people would only talk to her first, she would gladly talk to them), or uninterested in organizing lame school dances, or building one more tired-ass papier-mâché volcano for the science fair. (In fact, Eric Ritter's project had been a compelling dissertation on his working theory that DNA samples could be used forensically in any number of ways, which the sixteen-year-old would later regret was left unpublished.) An after-school date on this day includes a recap of the day's travesties and some solace in the distraction of *Father Knows Best,* unfortunately negated when some kid grabs Charlotte Anne's bus pass on 86th Street and C.P.W. and heads west to trade it for maybe a loose joint, only to be chased by an irritated Charlotte Anne, who is generally no kind of vigilante but is bigger than her would-be mugger by about a head, snatching the bus pass back in front of a bunch of stoop hangers on 87th who laugh and cheer. This small victory goes essentially unnoticed by Charlotte Anne — still bitter on behalf of Jenna, who she feels is misguided in feeling only disappointment this day — as she heads home to call Jenna about the near-mugging and make one more effort to convince her friend to share the rage. Jenna has come to believe that Charlotte Anne does have it together, praising her bravery by way of example, and Charlotte Anne appreciates that Jenna thinks this, even though she is secretly beginning to have doubts. Now that Charlotte Anne Byers has gathered some more information about Jenna Ritter, she's not any more sure than she was before that Jenna has it together, but has come to believe that Jenna has some non-potsmoking, overall fun and loyal qualities that a friend ought to have. As much as anything what it is is that Jenna's apparent optimism is so foreign to C.A. Byers as a worldview that she's hoping maybe at some point it'll catch.

Eleven

SHE'D BEEN SOBER A WHILE, but some things hadn't changed. Charlotte had heard it said many times in the program that A.A. wasn't a hotbed of mental health, but this hadn't stopped her from using it as a dating service. Early on it was a big draw. There were a lot of good-looking drunks, but around her sixth year of sobriety, after a particularly horrific date with yet another unmedicated bipolar alcoholic in which she felt compelled to hurl herself from the car about five minutes after he picked her up, she declared herself a born-again virgin and decided to wait until she fell in love, a risky proposition given that it hadn't happened once thus far. She had started to take baby steps toward her career goals but still struggled with the word *career.* Not to mention the word *goals.* Charlotte had interests but was never terribly *ambitious* (another word she had trouble with), and all three of these words seemed definitive. (And let's not even get started on the word *success,* because Charlotte has always thought something along the lines of How the hell do you define that? According to who? Sometimes if she was able to get out of bed before nine she felt her day was already an unqualified success.) She wanted to be a filmmaker, but what if she wanted to write a novel? What if she suddenly overcame her stage fright and learned how to play an instrument and got asked to sing backup for Tenacious D? How could she say no to that, except what if her movie was opening the same night as the Tenacious D tour and she had to decide between the two? Couldn't you sing backup for Tenacious D and also be a filmmaker? Who decided that you couldn't? Someone who was too tired to figure out what to call someone who was a filmmaking backup singer? Why did *career* have to imply only one thing? Why did *goals* seem to imply an end? What happens if you meet all your goals? Do you like, shoot off into space or something and burst into a worldwide fireworks display announcing goal completion and then cease to exist? What if she became completely disenchanted with anything remotely related to art or entertainment and suddenly became obsessed with backgammon? What if the CIA called and the CIA said, *We have a job that we think only you can do?* What if she stumbled into Baskin Robbins one day and felt a calling?

So it was that Charlotte prayed to the god of her "understanding" (quotes because her understanding had to date been so murky) that she would maybe calm down about the career/goals/ ambition thing long enough to make something happen in at least one of these fields and that she would be open to meeting someone relatively normal who would make her want to stay in the car (and that she would even recognize someone relatively normal if he crossed her path). Although she did not belong to any religion, she had heard various interpretations of the eleventh step over the years about what it was okay to pray for (the eleventh step of Alcoholics Anonymous suggests praying only for knowledge of god's will, but it also suggests meditation, which to Charlotte went as far as turning off the TV), i.e., go ahead and pray for whatever you want but it might be a better idea to pray only for god's will. Charlotte tended to struggle with this as she found it difficult to avoid the idea that god's will for everyone was to give up all material possessions and head for the farthest starving or war-torn country, not considering that maybe god, if he had a mind, and if he were a he and if he were only concerned with this sort of altruism, maybe had some more appropriate type of service in his mind for Charlotte, like maybe making a film that would compel millions of people to go out and do his will, which only muddles things a little more for Charlotte because she'd really rather make a film that would inspire people however it inspired them, but also because she wonders how she'd necessarily even know if she were making a film that inspired anyone at all, whether to do god's will or whatever else, or if it matters if she knows, which is often the real question she has about god's will, whether she prays for it or not, does it even matter if she knows, if it's being done anyway, and what about if god really is punishing, what if she's completely wrong about god insofar as the one thing she holds to is that god has to want what's good, even if she might not know what that is above and beyond generally treating people well. Further suggestions she's heard about prayer are that if you absolutely have to get specific, it's not a bad idea to pray for other people, particularly if you have resentments toward them (which gets into a weird area during moments when Charlotte's resentment is actually toward god), or for world peace, or the good health and fortune of loved ones (which gets into a very long list that Charlotte had to write down because she couldn't remember everyone and was always adding people so that it became a list of everyone she'd ever known to the point where her prayers started taking forty-five minutes every night and she fell asleep saying them, after which she decided god had to know who she loved without her reading off the list on a daily basis), things like this, which Charlotte did, but her logic was that if god wasn't answering those prayers, he may as well not answer a few more. It was like reverse psychology, but on god, which is both absurd and pathetic, but such was the state of Charlotte's relationship with god at the time, a logic arrived upon after a seemingly unfair number of family members became stricken with one fatal illness or another. She was aware that prayers for things like work or romance tended to be aided by some sort of action on the part of the praying person, *Faith without works is dead,* as it were, as opposed to prayers for sick people or whatever, where it seems more obvious that while this is a nice thing to do, if you're not a doctor, but plenty of times even if you are a doctor, really you can only do so much to help sick people recover, and she hoped that if there was a god who had a mind, he might go, *All right, that person has suffered enough, and you guys have been asking so nicely* or whatever. This actually made sense to her, sometimes, until these ridiculous numbers of relatives started getting sick, and then, not so much, but she kept asking, because, if nothing else, it seemed unlikely to hurt.

So after the prayer, Charlotte became friendly with this guy Russell, who she saw at first as just a friend, a very casual friend, someone she was getting to know in a strictly platonic, see-you-at-the-next-party kind of thing. It went on like that for a few months and she felt certain that there was no attraction of any kind, because of his overall style (big thick sweaters she might have really liked in 1990) and because of his overall looks (cute enough but not in a way that personally appealed to her at all) and because of his overall having a regular job and especially because of his overall political views, which she understood to be slightly right-leaning, and although this led to some lively conversations, Charlotte felt that there was no way she could ever be involved with someone who planned to vote for a candidate who had an overall demeanor not unlike that of a four-year-old who just found out he was getting skipped into second grade. When the election came, Russell admitted to having come to his senses and changing his vote, for a candidate who was at least smart, if not necessarily more promising, which brings up a lesser-of-two-evils sort of issue, not that it would matter in the end anyway, in any case, Russell's vote change served as his reentry into a genus of people she could in some theoretical universe date, as opposed to someone she could in no universe of any kind date.

A few months went by where they passed at parties and such and exchanged occasional hello or goodbye hugs but overall Charlotte still wasn't feeling him (and therefore, she hadn't really been taking any kind of notes on whether or not he was feeling her) and went about her business and then one day at another party Russell made a comment to Charlotte about how she struck him as being really kind of healthy, in an emotional way, which wasn't completely surprising — she knew she was fairly adroit at making people think she had it going on in that way (which gets into another whole thing about whether that was really a useful trait, which in fact she was pretty sure it wasn't, considering that maybe she could actually get some help from people, if she were willing to admit she needed any). Still, it was nice to hear, and had the effect of transforming Russell somewhat suddenly into possibly being a new and nice type. Possibly a normal type. Possibly the type she had prayed for. His niceness very suddenly transformed him into being someone she might ever want to kiss; it became a desirable quality to her, the niceness, and she felt that whether or not anything even took place with the nice possibly normal type, that she could possibly like some other normal type. The follow-ing day she received news that her first film had been financed, which, recall, she had also prayed for, and while Charlotte was not fully convinced that her prayers were directly related to these events, seeing as how she did take the necessary action to put the career success in order (i.e., writing the script, sending out the script, enduring many rejections of the script, rewriting the script, resubmitting the script, enduring several more rejections of the script, considering financing the script with her own money, remembering she had no money, submitting the script again, simultaneously fetching lots of coffee on lots of movie sets for lots of people until the financing finally came through), it cer-tainly encouraged her as far as any other prayers possibly coming true, it certainly caused her to consider praying for the perfect coffee table and maybe also a little less post–El Niño snow, which seemed reasonable considering that it would be harder for her to get out and do god's work if she couldn't get out at all, even though really, she was still never entirely sure of what sort of work it was she was supposed to be doing for god, and overall, although the seeming results of the prayers were pleasant, it still didn't do much to pinpoint her understanding of god, which continued to be fuzzy. (Including: capitalize, or no? What about the gender issue? Male? Female? Other? Why am I here? Are you in touch with my mom by any chance? Like this.)

At a Christmas party the following week, Charlotte was still having trouble gauging the level/nature of Russell's interest in her in terms of whether it was merely friendly or anything potentially more fun than merely friendly. She asked him questions about his work (he had one of those jobs that defy any description Charlotte could wrap her mind around), and although she was sincerely interested she also had her very good news to break and so she said, *Okay it's time to talk about me now I have good news,* and she told him the news and he was appropriately impressed and appeared to be overall present and accounted for in the conversation while obviously not suffering from any form of mania.

They had some lengthy and informative conversation about their families wherein it was uncovered that they had a few things in common, enough for a potential understanding but not so much that it was freaky and therefore causing them to have that premature intense soul-mate thing imperative in most of Charlotte's past relationships, which never failed to burn out within sixty to ninety days, which almost always resulted in vehement denial by one party or the other, but never both, that there was ever an intense soul-mate thing going on in the first place. Russell had five actual and whole siblings all from the same parents; Charlotte, as an only child, with a stepfamily that grew up in a different home, found this information to be almost impossible to process.

You mean like the Brady Bunch?

Same number of kids, but you may recall they were steps.

Like the Nelsons?

A little less happy. More kids.

Like the von Trapps?

Without the singing or Christopher Plummer plus some drinking. You have no frame of reference for this based in reality, do you?

I really don't.

This is where the story kind of drops off.

They never went out.

They ran into each other a few more times and continued flirting but that was about it until Charlotte said, *Okay, let's move it along or just be friends,* which was arguably a preemptive strike (and possibly indicative of progress on her part at least inasmuch as she tended to wait for them to bail on their own). At one point there was an elaborate fantasy sequence here, in which Charlotte and Russell start dating, and he starts wearing better sweaters, and better than that tolerates all her many weirdnesses (including varieties of meltdowns about things she can't control, which is possibly everything but let's just list here things such as trains that are very very late or leftover soup containers that won't open while somehow releasing a considerable amount of soup onto the counter, which she then has to throw on the floor, or accidentally breaking the last saucer from the set of dishes her parents bought in Ger-

many when they first married [the likes of which can tend her
into a total tailspin because she rarely breaks things and in spite of
the fact that her inventory of Mom/Dad related memorabilia is
vast, as well as being distributed across several states, that short of
some nationwide natural disaster there will never be a deficit,
although to continue the tangent and also to get back to the original idea, each of these little saucer-type losses tends to remind her
that one of the Mom/Dad people is gone, which decreasing physical evidence thereof makes her worry that she'll forget, which
seems to come under the heading of things not in her control,
which worry is arguably needless because she seems in no imminent danger of forgetting, presence or absence of evidence
notwithstanding], or people telling her to pray for god's will and
exactly how and then won't let it go until long after her ability to
be polite disappears and she has to yell at them [the whole on-
your-knees thing has been another source of god-related angst for
Charlotte, who wants to believe in a god you can talk to in any
position]). And what if you disagree with god about what's good
and he punishes you and let's say her worst fears are true about
that, like that the entire explanation for her disastrous love life to
date is that she broke up with nice guy Eddie Greenfield in high
school and god was like, *I gave you a nice one, see how you like this* kind-
of-thing. Or worse, possible punishments having to do with her
parents getting sick and exactly what Charlotte might have done
to cause that, and it seemed pretty obvious that she hadn't done
anything to cause these things to happen, especially with regard to
her dad, who wasn't one to worry about things when sometimes

there was cause for worry, e.g., not going to the doctor for seven years because he just forgot was his excuse (and also because he was constantly saying, *I'm going to live to be a hundred like my parents*, mostly meaning to be funny but kind of thinking he really would, and why wouldn't he, except they for sure went to the doctor), and then coming down with prostate cancer, and then Charlotte having to not yell at him because it's not really a good thing to yell at someone after they've gotten cancer, especially considering she thinks she should take some blame, since she would have told him to go to the doctor if she had known he had forgotten to go to the doctor, which she should have somehow psychically known, anyway now she yells at him to ask the doctor questions, which he doesn't like to do because he doesn't like to bother people, which also makes her want to yell at him, which she tones down to writing e-mails in big capital letters and making sure to say how much she loves him and wants him to stick around but which she's very glad she did because in the course of this he was also diagnosed with Parkinson's disease, which he wouldn't have known about if he hadn't gotten the cancer probably, which brings up the whole confusing everything-happens-for-a-reason issue, which tends to cause her brain to fly out of her head, because of course she

    a) wants to know the reason

and

    b) can always come up with too many possible reasons
          and then how do you know which one it is,

and most of all because

c) such a similar thing had happened with her mom
    insofar as she only discovered she had the cancer after
    breaking her hip, which at the time seemed to be
    happening for the reason that maybe they could cure
    the cancer, which they couldn't, and ultimately leaving
    the e.h.f.a.r. issue as murky as ever, unless you consider
    the one and only thing that makes the concept at all
    palatable for Charlotte which is that maybe she
    doesn't always get to know the reason, which it should
    be clear now is particularly problematic for her as she
    has always been extremely fond of the question *Why?*
    in spite of the probability of its ever being answered to
    her satisfaction. (Plus she never forgot what she heard
    at a meeting one time, where this issue is regularly
    debated, although Charlotte perceives a disconcerting
    weight on the pro side, in any case, the dude said, *Well,
    I don't know if everything happens for a reason but I know that
    everything does happen.* Point taken by Charlotte that since
    it's kind of up to the individual to elicit meaning from
    any given [sucky] thing, it might be useful to extract
    something positive, to do you-know-what with the
    lemons, as it were.) Recently she watched this whole
    episode of *Nova* about string theory and of course
    really didn't understand any of it except for the vague
    idea that there are, theoretically, these tiny little
    universes, strings or whatever, inside of the inside of
    the inside of atoms, more or less, is the best she can
    explain it, except as she's watching it she wonders why

none of these genius string-theorizing scientists on the show bother to bring up the issue of god, or any other unanswerable questions, like okay, it's great and all that you've discovered this limitless space where millions of tiny little people could be living, tiny little people we could be walking around crushing with our slippers without ever even knowing it, but of course there's no more proof of this, except for a whole bunch of equations and theorems or what have you, than there is of god, and it seems to Charlotte like someone ought to be mentioning that in spite of how spectacular this all is, the very fact that it's unprovable might indicate something bigger and more spectacular still, than even, you know, science. Anyway, you're probably better off if we save for another story all the illnesses her stepfather's been through since her mother died, which are equal in number and gravity, about which you can believe many more prayers were said. Why it's only occurring to her now to wonder whether this is all in vain is a mystery considering that there was evidence going back as far as when she was maybe seven and had prayed that her dad would come to New York because she hadn't seen him since she and her mom moved, and then he actually showed up at her school, but it was kind of terrible because he wasn't really supposed to see her, he was only there for a meeting with the lawyers, and she had to promise not to say anything to her mother in case she got

upset, which was pretty much a guarantee, and so
saying goodbye to her dad ended up being arguably
worse than if she'd never seen him at all, and so then
she had the thought, at seven, to pray even more
specifically, for her dad to come to New York so they
could actually spend time together, and then about
eight years went by in which she stopped thinking
about god at all and needless to say forgot about the
prayer until this whole weird incident in which she got
a late-night call from her friend Jenna asking if she
was okay, and saying of course she was okay and why,
and Jenna saying, *Because your dad called here from O'Hare
asking what was going on at your house — he said you called him
all upset and wanting him to come get you* (which was both
like her dad insofar as he didn't question things
sometimes and not at all like her dad insofar as he had
no tendency to be impulsive), and Charlotte/then
Charlotte Anne Byers saying she never called him and
telling Jenna to tell her dad to call her directly if he
called her back and not bothering to ask why he didn't
just call her instead of the Ritters, which she figured
was both because he thought she was in some bad
trouble and also because as a rule he rarely called
Charlotte/C.A.'s apartment, mostly so that he didn't
have to talk to C./C.A.'s mother, and also because he
thought he already spoke to her, which was kind of
fascinating and marginally irritating to Charlotte/
Charlotte Anne because she couldn't imagine how he

didn't know it wasn't her voice, which he later
explained was because the girl was so upset it was hard
to tell who it was. When her dad did call just a little
while later she told him it wasn't her and she was fine
and he should go home and even though he sounded
so sad and tired, Charlotte/C.A. Byers didn't quite
know what to think until just this moment remembering it, when she looks back on it kind of heartbroken
for both of them for having lost a whole bunch of
years together not to mention having prayed he'd
come to New York not once but twice and having it
turn out poorly both times. Suffice it to say all this
has messed her up with regard to prayer, and she has
experimented with it over the years, ranging from *Help*
to the long and involved prayers, although surprisingly
she only stopped praying altogether during one brief
period when she heard maybe the most heartbreaking
news she'd ever heard (unrelated to family members
for a change) and said to god, *Fuck you, god. Fuck. You. I*
don't even know why I curse you, god, considering you're not even
there. But fuck you anyway. I'm done. You know where to find me.
That was her last prayer for about two weeks. Which
turned out to be an interesting experiment because at
the end of the two weeks she felt really sad about the
idea of not believing in god at all and decided she'd
rather commit to acting like there was a good god
than act like there was no god at all, because think
about it, how could that hurt, even if you don't know

what it is, and who does, really, Charlotte wonders, with any certainty, it seems like the whole idea behind faith is that it requires faith, that doubt is almost a critical element of faith, really, at least a little doubt, otherwise it would be called certainty, and so it seems generally more useful to believe in something good that you aren't certain of than in something bad, or in nothing, and so at this point you can see how the thinking is maybe not terribly productive with regard to god, that said, she does believe in something, she feels pretty good about god when she's staring at the sky sort of just past dusk but more convinced if the wind's blowing, and she's well aware of the hokiness of god being in the wind, it's not whispering to her or anything, and yet regardless of the hokiness, does seem like it's a good representation of this thing you can't see but yet you can, can't touch but you can feel it comfort-type thing.

Not forgetting that we started with a fantasy, Russell eventually discovers she's not as healthy as he originally imagined her to be (see ¶ above), and it turns out that her character flaws aren't anything as wholly intolerable as she secretly fears but are in fact somewhat run-of-the-mill, which is curiously a little bit of a disappointment to her. Anyway so in the fantasy they move in together and everything's great and he proposes but there's a whole weirdness starting with the ring, basically what happens is it turns out to be his ex-fiancée's ring, which freaks her out until she finds out that it was also his mother's ring, and so they still almost get married, until he becomes kind of wiggly and then fades out at the altar and it turns out that he's a mirage. This sequence was ultimately rejected because Charlotte decided she wanted one of her fantasy sequences to go right for a change. So she decided to pray for a happier fantasy, that maybe it would help her to go a step backward and pray to just be able to have a happy fantasy before she prayed for a real and actual normal guy, which gets back to the whole thing about praying for anything other than god's will, like work, or normal boyfriends, or even for the interest in having and/or willingness to have, or the ability to even recognize, a normal boyfriend, or dads coming to visit, because it might have been noted earlier that prayers like this frequently come with the same warning, the essence of the reason why you're supposed to pray for god's will, which at least in theory is better than anything you might think to ask for, which is be careful what you wish for. That being said, given both her recent good fortune and that she seemed to have at least gotten the willingness part, with regard to the normal thing, she had reason to hope that at some point her prayers might come true.

Brooklyn

Dateless CHARLOTTE ANNE BYERS attributes her condition to her old-fashioned name and decides to drop the *Anne* the summer of her sixteenth year. At the beginning of her sophomore year, Charlotte Anne had made note that two girls in her class of forty-eight kids had come back to school with suspiciously modified noses, and she saw the name change as a less painful makeover. Plus, it was the dawning of the age of disco and seemed time for a change. However, in what she will later refer to as "a freak renaming accident," Charlotte somehow mutated into Charlie (which she was no longer so enamored of as she had been when she was eight), and a permanent name change to Charlotte would only take hold several years in the future, after her college graduation, when she stubbornly refused to answer to anything else.

Newly renamed Charlie Byers has officially been best (all-around) friends with Jenna Ritter since the middle of seventh grade, when she was still Charlotte Anne and when Jenna, faring poorly in French class, was assigned to be Charlotte Anne's French "buddy." Though Jenna will in following years report teasingly about what Charlotte Anne refers to as a "hesitation" to get involved with such a project, Charlotte Anne stands by her story that it was not true that Jenna's first call to Charlotte Anne was greeted with a petulant "What?" It could be said that Charlotte Anne had some idea that she was cooler than Jenna, which opinion would likely not have been corroborated by anyone else in their seventh-grade class, and any vague possibility of truth in that notion would be erased after Charlotte Anne accidentally became Charlie and Jenna cut her hair into wings.

Jenna gets a lot of dates this fall, and the newly monikered Charlie, through no fault of Jenna's, quickly becomes known as Jenna's sidekick, which, considering how graciously she'd taken Jenna on in the first place, Charlotte Anne/Charlie bitterly resents (privately — in grade school, C.A./C. Byers had, in an effort to prevent anyone else from going away, perfected hiding a broad range of feelings when her parents divorced, and after an initial three-week nonstop crying jag, ceased crying altogether). Her resentment is not so much directed toward Jenna as it is toward the rest of the sophomore class, who, taken with Jenna's makeover and possibly also by her ceaselessly friendly demeanor, naturally assume that Charlotte Anne/Charlie is some kind of charity case, or at least is a testament to Jenna's boundless goodwill, seeing as how Jenna and Charlotte Anne/Charlie both have the good sense to keep it to themselves that they still spend a lot of Saturday nights at home watching *Donny & Marie* as late as their senior year (by which time Charlotte Anne will mercifully have had her own makeover, cutting bangs [which will be her signature hairstyle for the next fourteen years], losing fifteen life-changing pounds, and miraculously and simultaneously being the first girl in school to wear Calvin Klein jeans [nothing more than good luck and in no way indicative of any kind of trendsetting on her part]) while the rest of their class (anyone not at the Central Park band shell getting stoned) watches *The Midnight Special*.

By midwinter of their sophomore year, Jenna Ritter is going out with senior Tim Flaherty, unquestionably the cutest guy to hit their high school since the two Dougs (Greenberg and Stein) graduated the year before. Tim is a little different, though. Tim is from Brooklyn, imported due to his strength as a swimmer, and his excellence in sports and good cheekbones propelled him to the highest levels of popularity available at Davis Academy (small class size and the lack of a football team [and mercifully, the lack of cheerleaders] seem to prohibit the typically vast divisions between cliques seen in larger high schools, and though there are two significant distinctions in the class of "parkies" [who go to the park and get stoned] and everyone else, the lines are often blurred, because otherwise the parties would be too small). Tim is really cute but it would be an understatement to say that Jenna is significantly smarter. But even among Upper West Side high schoolers who fancy themselves rather sophisticated in spite of their continued *Donny & Marie* watching, *smart* is way down on the list of desirable boyfriend qualities. Tim can do the hustle.

And actually, Charlotte Anne/Charlie attributes Tim's sweet personality to his lesser intelligence and appreciates that he does not consider her to be Jenna's (inferior) sidekick, engaging in conversation with her on the rare occasion that she and Jenna are not conjoined (a condition fostered by both girls in entirely individual fashion — for reasons never understood by Charlotte Anne, Jenna will go out of her way to get them to dress like twins, and it did happen that on occasion they would purchase identical or similar items accidentally [or on purpose with an agreement to forewarn the other if one was planning to wear it any given day], but the truth is that Jenna will sometimes purposely wear the duplicate garment in spite of the agreement, to Charlotte Anne's great embarrassment, and if the idea of sixteen-year-olds dressing alike weren't bad enough, it is always Charlotte Anne who's accused of being the copier. Charlotte Anne/Charlie drew up a written agreement after about the fourth twin-dressing incident, but Jenna refused to sign, and Charlotte Anne was forced to retire several favorite items from her wardrobe). She had also taken to registering for as many of the same classes as Jenna as she possibly could, with the exception of AP Bio, which she would have absolutely failed. (Plus, in spite of being no particular kind of animal activist, C.A. has a low tolerance for dissection of any kind.) Such is Tim Flaherty's kindness that he eventually relays to Charlie Byers (via Jenna Ritter) that he has a friend in Brooklyn asking if Jenna has any cute friends to fix him up with. Tim calls Jenna who calls Charlotte Anne who reluctantly agrees to a blind date.

Several more rounds of phone calls occur negotiating the terms and conditions of the date. The date will take place in Brooklyn, which outer borough Charlotte Anne had rarely traversed. Both girls have long-standing and to their minds completely reasonable reservations about hanging out east of Central Park, north of 96th Street, or south of the Village, and the latter only occasionally. They are Upper West Siders and see no good reason to leave. (Jenna does not make any effort to deny that she was in fact born in Brooklyn, but prior to the season of Tim had not returned since her family moved to Manhattan ten years before.) Fortunately for Tim Flaherty and his friend Chuck Farley, due to the recent release of *Saturday Night Fever,* Brooklyn has an exotic cachet as the home of disco, and Jenna and Charlotte Anne are not above the occasional adventure into foreign boroughs, especially when the possibility of dates is present.

Also covered in the dating negotiations is mode of dress (casual), transportation (Jenna's parents will drive them to Brooklyn, the boys will drive them home), and does Charlie have any reservations about Chuck Farley having one testicle. (*No she does not;* Charlotte Anne tells Jenna who tells Tim who tells Chuck that it will be no problem at all that he has one testicle because at no time will she be making contact with or even viewing any number of testicles, that evening or soon thereafter; that he could have as many testicles as could possibly be concealed under his Sergio Valentes without suggesting themselves to her in any way. Charlotte Anne never gets an exact transcript of the agreement relayed back to Chuck Farley but suspects Tim was not that explicit.)

Charlotte Anne plans to sleep over at Jenna's when they get back that night and has the foresight to bring two choices of outfits just in case Jenna is planning to argue that dressing like twins just this one night would be perfectly fine, seeing as how they'd be in Brooklyn, bringing two choices Jenna couldn't duplicate anyway, finally selecting a gray cashmere V-neck sweater she'd gotten on sale in the men's department at Charivari. (The Calvins are, at this point, a given.) Jenna wears a pair of slightly flared jeans with heart-shaped back pockets (also owned by C.A.), a maroon Danskin leotard, and a cotton plaid shirt tied at the waist, a style she claims to have pioneered in spite of a very well-known photograph depicting Marilyn Monroe in a tied-up gingham shirt, which Charlotte Anne suspects Marilyn Monroe herself did not pioneer. (Jenna would subsequently begin a lifelong practice of almost patenting things, and gets a little better at it over the years, almost patenting the E-ZPass.) Neither Charlotte Anne/Charlie nor Jenna wears a lot of makeup, but Bonnie Bell Lip Smackers are an indispensable enhancement to their natural beauty. (During a rerun of *Donny & Marie*, they had rated all the girls in their class on a scale from "excellent" to "fair" and were the only ones in the "excellent" category while most fell off the scale into "poor," never questioning that they might not be home on a majority of Saturday nights watching *Donny & Marie* if their excellence were universally recognized, always maintaining among themselves that they did so "by choice." And that they knew perfectly well that their excellence was not universally recognized, and that it was a travesty. Anyone with any objectivity [not any of the girls] might argue that Melissa Myers is the prettiest girl in the class, but at 5'11" she wears stiletto heels to school on a daily basis, in spite of most of their classes being conducted on the fourth or fifth floor of a walk-up, and her senior quote will read "Too bad I'm just naturally better than all of you," which doesn't do much to endear her to anyone outside of Studio 54 and thereby detracts from her looks somewhat.)

After a minor fender bender en route to Brooklyn, Dr. and Mrs. Ritter wait outside the Flahertys' modest row house in Canarsie until the girls wave goodbye, ushered in by an elderly woman in a housedress.

"The boys will be right up," the woman says, seating herself on a well-worn recliner next to a TV tray cluttered with used tissues and crossword-puzzle books. "They're just down in the rec room fixing up. Tissue?" The housecoated woman offers the Daitch-brand box in their direction. Tim Flaherty and Chuck Farley ascend from the basement smiling at the girls sleepily. Tim has naturally kind of small eyes, but there is no question even for the uninitiated Charlotte Anne that the boys are stoned. At this point, Charlotte Anne/Charlie Byers and Jenna Ritter are adamantly anti-drug (Charlotte Anne presently having no idea that college will end up being vastly more unpleasant socially than high school and that she will begin abusing alcohol and some downers almost immediately upon moving into her freshman dorm) and pride themselves on being "together" and having no need to alter their minds in that sort of way. (Charlotte Anne, two Thanksgivings prior, had had the unfortunate experience of having dinner at her stepgrandparents' house in the Bronx; while meals there were always spectacular displays of Italian American cooking, on this particular occasion her stepfather's cousin produced a marijuana cigarette, inviting all present, including Charlotte Anne, her mother and stepfather, the stepgrandparents, his mother, and his twelve-year-old son, to partake of the substance. Charlotte Anne, her young stepcousin [removed some number of times, she never knew how people calculated that], and step-great-aunt declined, and the ensuing dinner was an embarrassment from which she would never fully recover. Highlights from the evening included her stepgrandfather dismissing the effects of the substance entirely on the basis of his being a hard-core nicotine addict, his wife getting the giggles and wondering aloud why she hadn't tried it sooner, saying, "Pass the *bracciola*," Charlotte Anne's mother getting the giggles and hugging her daughter a lot, and the step-great-aunt running back and forth from the kitchen screaming, "You're all going to get brain damage," "How could you offer that to my grandson!" and "You need help! All of you!" Charlotte Anne was of a similar mind as her step-great-aunt except for the brain-damage part [further enhancing her misery was that her mother and stepfather made some issue about her being "uptight," urging her to "get loose," which created a nearly uncontainable rage inside her], but sat in stunned silence with her head practically in her broccoli rabe, wondering how she ended up in some disastrous reverse of what was actually supposed to be going on with teenagers, and ruing her earlier decision to stay off drugs as having led directly to this weird reversal, although she did not feel, at the time, that partaking of the Thanksgiving marijuana with her family would stun them into a reverse reversal whereby they would be transformed into parents who punish their kids for doing drugs and getting bad grades and having sex or whatever. Sixteen-year-old Charlotte Anne Byers is certain that her destiny as the only child of the most bizarre family anywhere has been set, and that she has no alternative but to hold fast to her previous anti–drug/sex/swearing stance [the latter of which is also rampant in her household], which lasts until about her second week of college.) Mind-altering, in conjunction with Chuck Farley's non–Tim Flaherty–resembling-in-any-way looks, does not bode well for romance. Chuck Farley is neither hideous nor outstanding, and to his benefit he is wearing brown jeans and a Shetland sweater, the only evidence of his disco orientation being a pair of marshmallow shoes — brown vinyl with white platform soles — but unfortunately for him, C.A. Byers has had a lifelong big thing about bad shoes, the wearing of which she finds personality-telling and worse for Chuck Farley, in this particular instance, than having one testicle. Tim is actually wearing white flared polyester pants and a black shirt with four or five buttons open, redeemed only by his not having any visible chest hair, and his being super cute.

"You look sleepy, son," the woman says to Tim. "Have a tissue."

"I'm okay, thanks, Grandma. You met the girls?" The woman in the housedress nods, wipes her nose, and goes back to her crossword puzzles.

The dates retreat to the rec room to discuss plans and the boys offer Jenna and Charlie a joint, which they decline, miraculously in this case not leading to a conversation about why they don't get high; Charlotte Anne suspects that in the history of high school there has never been a conversation about why anyone *does* get high, and has learned from experience that when declining drugs it's always best to act like you were already stoned (an uncomfortable incident at a pot party the year before in which she had actually said, "No thank you," to a joint passed her way by Clarisse Benjamin resulted in a roomful of laughter, indicating to Charlotte Anne that manners were an inappropriate formality in the pot-smoking universe and that in the future some sort of lie would work best), or that you were hungover and therefore had a solid reason for abstaining. Having to drive is a nonissue for the unlicensed Charlotte Anne/Charlie and Jenna, but it's a questionable excuse anyway, since C.A./C. Byers knows that some potheads have a weird pride thing about driving better when stoned, which she thinks is a big bunch of bullshit that she generally opts not to challenge since challenging potheads tends to be a kind of *Who's On First* exercise in absurdity. Jenna and Tim quickly go out to get a paper to see what's playing, leaving Charlotte Anne alone in the basement with her stoned, platform-shoe-wearing date for the longest half hour of her life (which half hour is curious in and of itself since she'd noticed a newsstand on the corner when they got there, and notes, upon their return, a suspicious lack of Lip Smacker on Jenna Ritter's lips). Chuck Farley tries to ask her some questions about sports (one minute), some questions about what kind of music she likes (four minutes; he claims not to like disco [making the marshmallow shoes an even more inexplicable fashion choice] and puts on a Steppenwolf album that is harboring some pot seeds), some questions about college (two minutes — she will go wherever she gets in and he will go into the merchant marines with Tim. Charlotte Anne/Charlie really has no idea what the merchant marines are but doesn't ask), and some questions about what movie she wants to go see (two minutes — she wants to see *Annie Hall* and he wants to see *The Omen*, which divergent choices pretty much sum up the entire evening for her, not to mention she's thinking they could make a movie about his shoes called *The Omen*). After that they pretty much just sit and listen to Steppenwolf until Tim and Jenna come back, with Chuck occasionally air drumming along, glancing over to smile at Charlie during the air-drum solo, which causes her to wonder if this is some kind of Brooklyn dating ritual, since Chuck genuinely seems like he's meaning to impress her with the air drumming. Tim and Jenna have no newspaper in their possession, which is just as well if it means they don't have to sit through *The Omen*. Tim says, "Let's just go," which is not questioned by the girls, and they leave in Tim's white Firebird, the hood of which displays the Firebird's portrait. Charlotte Anne and Jenna, city girls (and there is no telling either of them that people from the outer boroughs are also entitled to describe themselves with the *city* adjective), are years away from obtaining driver's licenses and are therefore unfamiliar with the whole car-culture thing, but Charlotte Anne has a good idea she's supposed to be impressed with the Firebird even though she very much isn't.

About a half hour later, the girls, in the backseat, begin to realize that they're kind of just driving around, and Charlotte Anne musters the courage to ask where they're going. "We thought we'd just cruise," Tim says. "Did you want to go somewhere? Should we go get something to eat?"

Charlotte Anne/Charlie looks over to Jenna, who doesn't seem much like she's into driving around either. The appeal of cruising is lost on them, and due to their having just seen *Saturday Night Fever*, Charlotte Anne somehow imagines this ending with one of them hanging off the Brooklyn Bridge for "fun." "Okay," she says, and they drive around some more looking for a restaurant until she notices that the gas needle is on E and dares to point it out, hoping they'll stop at a gas station.

"Nah, it's fine," Tim says. "There's always a few gallons left when it's on empty."

"Let's stop anyway," Jenna says, having heard that line before and found herself stranded in Brooklyn more than once. Tim pulls into a gas station and Chuck hands him a single. Tim hands two singles to the gas-station attendant, who looks at him unsurprised and knowing he isn't going to get a big tip on the 2.4-gallon fill. They're about to pull away as soon as the needle budges slightly over to the right side of the E, but Chuck comes up with an idea. "Let's just eat here," he says. Charlotte Anne surveys the gas station for an adjoining restaurant. There are some vending machines. Tim hands him a dollar, and as Chuck opens the car door, he spies a fat wallet lying on the ground. "Alriiiight!" he says, showing the wallet to Tim with a celebratory air drum. "Dinner aborted. Let's go shopping!" Chuck pulls out twenty dollars and a BankAmericard. Jenna, never one to cause controversy but whose good moral standards will not, like Charlotte Anne's, be corrupted for most of the eighties into drink, says, "No. Give it to me. We have to give it back." The boys laugh at first, but there is no doubt that their chances of any action with the girls that night will be drastically reduced if they don't (although sadly for Chuck, his chances couldn't be lower than they already are), and Tim places the wallet in Jenna's care.

Cruising continues for another hour, Charlotte Anne seeing no sights or particular activity that will enhance Brooklyn or Chuck Farley's chances with her in any way (Chuck's expression of disappointment in not happening on a fight or even a fender bender will finally seal this deal against him), and the shoes, the wallet scandal, and the dollars plus her having figured out that her married name would be Charlie Farley, that they'd be Chuck and Charlie Farley, end his chances of ever seeing her again and result in a temporary restoration of Charlotte Anne Byers's original name. The boys finally drop the girls back in the city around quarter to one, Charlotte Anne thrusting her hand toward Chuck's to avert a kiss, the trajectory of which she can't be certain. Chuck Farley calls several times to ask her out again, which she dodges by saying she has plans until she's eventually able to bring herself to lie and tell him she's seeing someone else. The following year, after she has her "real" first date, with Eddie Greenfield, she will deny that the Brooklyn date ever took place.

✦

All This Heavenly Glory

✦

SO IT TURNS OUT that he's depressed. This was not on the list I came up with when I imagined, over the last two months, all the many reasons he rejected me and all the many reasons everyone has ever rejected me, and when I say many I am meaning to say very many, none good, really, none involving much in the way of anything having to do with the other person, all involving me being essentially unlovable and ending with me trying to reconcile this, the fact of my unlovability, since there is no possible chance that there is any other reason I have been rejected by him, and by everyone; why no one will ever come out and say that that's what it is is the ultimate unsolved mystery to me, because it seems to me like it would be so much more merciful if one honest representative for all men out there would once and for all admit the truth, maybe send out a form letter to say, *We are sorry, Charlotte Byers, but the reason we are not interested is because you are manifestly and singularly unlovable.*

But people seem to think it's better to say, *It's not you.* I don't know why anyone would think that's useful, because so often it is you, and if they would only admit that it is you, and if they could further explain in exactly what way it is you, it seems to me like they would ultimately be doing you a service, that if someone would say, *Charlotte, although you are presenting overt manifestations of classic physical beauty and are clearly pleasing to the untrained eye, you are in fact minus one or more of the following: moon-shaped freckles, night-blooming jasmine that sprouts from the crown of your head like a halo, bracelets of butterflies alit on your wrists, a laugh that emits diamond-studded soap bubbles; furthermore you do not drool on your pillow in the shape of puppy dogs, your leg hair does not grow into pleasing designs, you are minus a habit of making sculptures out of dripping candle wax so endearing that men will incur thousands of dollars of debt keeping you in candles, you are lacking the tendency to cause weekly fender benders due to mindlessly wiping your spilled chai tea from whatever you're wearing, additionally, I personally have a strong preference for a woman who sneezes like a Siamese kitten, so even if you drooled real puppy dogs I would not be interested,* then you could at least have some useful information, because if you were forced to accept that you will simply never drool in a desirable way, that when you were born, you were genetically defective in this one area, unalterable by any available chemical compound or by psychotherapeutic, medical, or holistic treatment of any kind, that it is something that you simply must accept as immutable fact, then you might possibly, if you have any interest, be able to take it as a loss and attempt to enjoy the other, non-romantic parts of your life.

But this won't happen. What happens instead is that they make excuses. Sometimes, as here, the excuse is in some part or is even entirely true, but is still an excuse, an extensive but true back-story set forth some time later at a length of several hours over coffee, the primary goal of which is still to avoid saying that it is me, and the whole unlovable thing.

✻   ✻   ✻

So unhhh. It was the most debilitating crush I'd had in years. It had been so many years, in fact, that I thought, in the best way, that it might never happen again. It had only happened a handful of times, but the results were always so devastating that I hoped it would never happen again. Or I hoped it would be entirely different than what I thought it was. It seemed like something I should have been able to control, and I thought I actually had controlled, and then I met Matteo, and it became clear that it wasn't controlled, that it was only lying dormant, accelerating like a tailgater who isn't even late, without my knowledge. I'd been dating but hadn't had any strong feelings about anyone in such a long time that I'd been thinking I never would. Considering what I knew about him, which was more or less nothing, it was essentially inexplicable. We had met briefly about a year before at a garage sale at my friends Janet and Tony's place. Matteo, a friend of Tony's, stopped by to say hi, and I can't say I was overwhelmed at that point, but I did think, He could be cute. I tried and failed to get Tony to fix us up once or twice after that, and Tony didn't say he wouldn't, but he also said that Matteo had just broken up with someone and it might not be the best time. I eventually forgot about it.

Almost a year later I saw him again at Janet and Tony's wedding. It was one of those marvelous and rare weddings where you know the couple is really in love but you also know them both well enough to know that it's not some fairy tale, that they're two real people with problems like anybody else who've worked pretty hard to be together. Janet and Tony had asked people in advance to participate in the ceremony in any way they cared to as long as it was about love, which was something of a struggle for me, since what I know about it isn't good, and about a day before the wedding I finally came up with something, the gist of which was, *Well what I know about love isn't good, but Janet and Tony give me hope.* After the ceremony a cute dark-haired guy came up to me and said we could probably have a long discussion about what we both didn't know about love, and I said, *Matteo?* because it had been so long I had forgotten what he looked like. I still wasn't sure how cute he was to me, although anyone in a nice suit and a gardenia in his lapel bumps up a little, but later I saw him on the dance floor. In retrospect I should have probably hurled myself from the bell tower of the church right then. Instead we danced and I made attempts at flirting and he was still dancing when I left so I told Tony to give him my number. Not entirely thought through since Tony and Janet were about to go on their honeymoon.

Tony and Janet went on and came back from their honeymoon and over the course of several weeks I asked Tony almost every time I saw him if he'd talked to Matteo; I got vague answers indicating that he did talk to Matteo but maybe not about me, which left me frustrated and eventually pretty bummed out. One morning I was driving home from the grocery store and I burst into tears about it for no reason that seemed relative to the eleven minutes I'd spent with him (based on that thing people say about grieving for a month for every year you've dated, this calculates to about forty-eight seconds of grieving time, and that's of course only if you allow for a generous definition of *dated*, so generous that it includes imaginary dating). And yet it suddenly struck me as tragic that Matteo and I weren't even getting a chance. I called Janet from my car right then, which if you know me you know is a big deal because driving's not my thing and the world is generally a safer place if I reserve the cell/car combo for emergencies, which is what it seemed like at the time, and I said, *Listen, I'm going to get Matteo's number and call him myself unless Tony gives me some good reason not to,* and Janet said, *Oh, Charlotte, I think that's a great idea,* and called me back with the number about an hour later. I planned something clever to say and left a message on Matteo's cell the next day. He called me right back. He was glad I called. He told me that it was the best message he'd ever gotten. That's what he said. We exchanged the most basic who-are-you and where-are-you-from information. He's second-generation Italian. His parents are from Italy, and, okay, I'm such a sucker, but Matteo spoke Italian before he spoke English and it came up not a few times that he had reason to say Italian things, with an impeccable Italian accent, but whatever, I went for it, and who wouldn't? I'm a first-generation New Yorker. (This never fails to produce an overly fascinated *Really?* which often, as in this case, implies a disbelief that anyone raised in the übercity would subsequently be inclined to make a lateral move to a place many consider both second to the übercity and also windy. I moved to Chicago primarily because New York got too expensive, but honestly, I love it here. Personally I don't find it to be second at all in any number of ways, not the least of which is that there are 5 or 6 million fewer people pressing up against me when I walk out my door.) He's working on a film right now. I have a film coming out. Tony hadn't even mentioned it. Matteo was impressed. We made plans and before we hung up, he said, *I feel like I really know you.*

Shut up. Just shut the fuck up. Yes, I know a warning sign when I see one, thank you very much. I have much experience in the way of people saying overly intense things way too soon. I wanted to be known. So fuck me. I'm not telling this story because it went well.

So we had this one date (which word usage he would later call into question, which is just, just, just, just give me that one little thing, we don't call up massively foxy dudes just to be buddies, or if we do we certainly don't leave them messages that indicate in no uncertain terms that we think they're massively foxy, and so in my estimation if you agree to a social outing with the calling person, no matter how casually construed, which in this case was a day-time walk on the beach, at the very least you have to know that the calling person is thinking it's a date, no matter what kind of denial you're in), and it was one of those dates that doesn't happen very often, not for me anyway, insofar as you start out physically attracted to someone and then it turns out that you actually have things in common, in this case he's a budding filmmaker, and I'm a filmmaker slightly past budding. He's also an actor (which admittedly I should have considered as a clue; even though I try not to draw conclusions based on any kind of stereotype, the fact is that I'd had considerable experience dating actors in New York, and that speaking in the most general terms, they were a lot who, while often bright and engaging and charming and funny and attractive, tended to think and talk about themselves at great length, and then I moved to Chicago where there isn't quite the multitude of actors that there is in New York, and although I still have actor friends, I find that I don't really miss them as part of the dating pool). In any case we had much to talk about, filmmaking and art and life and families and shoes even, the guy has a thing about shoes and shopping, so that when I told him I'd just bought a pair of very *Sex and the City* shoes, he said, *Tell me about them,* tell me about them, he said, understanding that there was a conversation to be had about a pair of shoes, which is not only rare but a major plus in my book, and I felt comfortable but excited and hopeful (the latter of which will later reveal itself to perhaps be the element of all this that is now and has always been killing me). If I am to be entirely honest, I was never 100 percent certain that the physical attraction was mutual, but I am not an idiot, and I know when, at the very least, I am making some kind of connection with someone, even if my radar about the rest of it is sometimes off. (Of course, sometimes it's obvious, people say romantic or flirty things or they kiss you or have sex with you or whatever, then there's no mystery, but the signs here were a little nebulous.) Anyway, I figured I'd find out next time, because at that point I was sure there'd be a next time. He told me that Tony hadn't said anything about me except that I don't make left turns (which isn't even altogether accurate, I make a lot of left turns, and although it would not be impossible to avoid left turns entirely, it would require an absurd amount of going out of the way; admittedly there are left turns I refuse to make, but it's more accurate to say that I don't like to make left turns, and that I am sometimes willing to go a little bit out of the way, when I feel my life is at stake, which here in Chicago comes up in a number of locations because there are these horrific six-way intersections all over town without left-turn signals where it's just a free-for-all of death risk, where you're I guess just expected to set yourself right in the middle of the massive intersection and hope for the best, and in my neighborhood I've figured out the shortest ways around these intersections, but unfortunately there are other neighborhoods I don't know as well where you think you can just go a block past the intersection and make a right and another right and another right again but you can't, you end up on a street with a river or a cemetery or an industrial park on the right that goes for a mile before there's anywhere safe for you to turn around, anyway, that said, it's not nearly as much of a problem for me as people think it is, and when I questioned him later, Tony said, *It seemed like the most telling thing I could think of,* which is, all right, it's a little bit funny but maybe isn't the thing to be telling someone in the event of a fix up, usually people say, *She's funny* or *She's bright* or *She just won an award at Sundance,* which seemed like the most obvious thing to me, since I had just won an award at Sundance, a screenwriting award for my film *All This Heavenly Glory* — you get the point, it's usually something good), anyway when he told me this I was at that moment rather stunned, unable to believe that that would be the thing anyone would tell someone about me, you know, as a selling point, but, and we're getting to the only possible compliment thing here, when I finally let him speak, Matteo said he thought it was *really cute.* (This is what I mean about it all being so nebulous in general as to what it is or isn't that people find attractive; personally I'm not even a little bit uncomfortable about the way I look, which is not to say that I think I'm the hottest thing ever, either, but nevertheless may be the only thing about me that I've ever been completely at ease with, and if you're interested in the psychology behind that I will happily further digress just long enough to tell you that it's fascinating to me, on a bigger-picture level, the way vast numbers of parents will try to do the opposite of what their parents did that they think fucked them up, only to leave the subsequent generation not healthier but fucked up in an entirely fresh way; in this case, my mother, who was quite beautiful, had not ever been told she was beautiful as a child, and I think she also wasn't told that she was loved very often, which you can imagine left her frequently depressed, and so I think she thought that if she told me every day, more than once a day, how beautiful I was and how much she loved me, that I would not suffer this fate as she did, and so although I felt beautiful and loved, this would also result in some persistent confusion about whether or not I was anything else, e.g., smart/talented/kind/whatever, or if I even needed to be, and as it turns out I did not get discovered by a superagent as I sauntered down the street, the virtual magic of my beauty propelling me into some sort of general superstardom, and it was probably during that phase when I realized that I should actually try to work for whatever sort of superstardom I was interested in, and then it took a few years after I quit drinking for me to remember what that even was, and then it was a few more years before I actually did, anyway the point is that when someone says something like this to you, that they think it's cute that you don't make left turns, it kind of highlights that total subjectivity of what anyone finds attractive, and of course in this case, as much as I find it fascinating that this would be the thing anyone would find cute about me, in the end it still seems to me that in and of itself it's not enough, the inability to make left turns, that this guy and for all I know every other guy I've ever been with has thought something along the lines of, *Well, she's cute, and she doesn't make left turns, but she's not from Kuala Lumpur.*) I'm just saying this was the only time the word *cute* or anything like it came up during the entire date, although there was a protracted hug, which I could also find ways to discount because he's Italian, and having my own Italian step-family, I know that they are often a warm and effusive and physical people, there is a lot of hugging and bold expressions of affection that are just part of who they are and not necessarily romantic (and yet, a guy like this, in my estimation, is smart enough to know that this is a thing he has going for him, and might conceivably use to his favor, whether or not he was even romantically interested in someone, do you know what I mean, he could not be interested in me but still secretly want me to be interested in him, which, honestly, if you want to know the truth, I recognize because it's a huge part of my own modus operandi, whether I'm interested or not, I for sure want you to find me desirable, although actually I don't think I usually try to actively solicit that, beyond wearing cute clothes and fixing my hair and wearing makeup, I mean, I'm not out there flirting with every single person, it's just what I hope, I want people to adore me whether or not I adore them — maybe that's some kind of pathology but I also think it's kind of just human). Anyway, when the date was over there was no definite plan for another date but the phrase *next time* was used several times and he totally said he had a great day and I had no reason not to believe him. He gave me an amazing hug and I'm sure I pulled away first because it was almost too much for me to take, but it wasn't until I got upstairs and was replaying it in my head that I realized he hadn't let me pull all the way away, that he'd left his hands on my waist while he was still talking, for an amount of time that in my estimation goes past friendly, plus it was my waist. Janet and Tony don't hug me like that. Tony doesn't even hug me at all. (He has a thing about men hugging women who aren't their wives, and you know what, on the surface it's kind of old-fashionedy but really, I totally get where Tony's coming from on that, now.) So Matteo had his hands on my waist and he asked for my number again because he lost his cell phone, *The worst part of which*, he said, *was losing your message.* He had been keeping my message. The best message he ever got.

And then of course, he never called. Well, technically he did call, but we never went out again as friends or anything else. (Not that I ever had any interest in being friends, I need one more male friend I've dated who eventually tells me about all the other women he loves like I need a spike through my skull.) Indulge me in providing the minutes of what followed and the calls that were exchanged (dates approximate):

Days 1–6: Call friends to discuss minutiae of date. Regrettably, mention it to dad in an e-mail. Write minutiae in journal. Enjoy afterglow. Program M.'s number into cell. Leave cell phone on 24/7 as he does not have home number.

Day 7: Continue hope that M. will call to make a weekend plan. Create fallback excuses for why he might not call, which include but are not limited to: He's busy working as a stand-in on a feature film. He went on location. He's sick. He's stuck in a giant spiderweb. He's been in a terrible elevator accident and due to a severe head trauma he's in the psych wing at Northwestern Memorial believing himself to be James VanDerBeek. He got three wishes from a genie but in his excitement didn't think it through and now he's tiny and lives in the genie bottle. He's been abducted by chain-smoking alien supermodels.

Day 9: Attempt to implement the more reasonable of the fall-back excuses.

Day 13: Have the first in a series of meltdowns of varying intensity and duration involving peak levels of self-hate that come as something of a surprise, as for many years up to this point, I have not been, thanks to years of therapy and twelve-step programs, relinquishing huge portions of my day to thoughts about my irreversible romantic deficiencies and their specifics, that in fact I have had any number of moments where it seemed a revelation, and as true as anything, that I had simply not met the right person. Speculate that Tony's hesitation to accelerate fix up was due to his belief that I do not have magnetic properties and that Matteo is looking for someone silverware will stick to.

Day 14: Call M., who reports that he's been busy making a short film for a festival that is to take place in about an hour. Invite self. Vacuum a friend into drama for support. Attempt to act casual, like we were on our way from there to the masked ball where we'd already planned to be but were just squeezing this in. (M.'s film, in which he also stars, is, wouldn't you know, about his obsession with a girl he can't have, a married bipolar chain-smoking West Indian model whose regular habit of accidentally setting their bedsheets on fire with her cigarette ashes makes him wild with desire, possessing him, in their brief relationship, to make love with her on the floor with the flaming bed next to them, which apparently is supposed to, you know, mean something, anyway the whole movie,

largely out of focus, is mostly just a tight shot of him talking into
the camera about his obsession with her, and the destructive nature
of the relationship, and how he's just broken up with her, running
his fingers through his dark, wavy, thick, magnificent hair and the
countless products it's hosting, and chain-smoking, dragging on his
Winstons as though she might be inside them, occasionally looking
around meaningfully, and then at the end, a slender brown hand
comes into the frame and takes his still-burning cigarette out of his
hand and flicks it behind him and the camera pulls back wide
enough so you see the entire West Indian girlfriend, who has been
on the floor waiting for him, and whose presence calls into question
the guy's concept of a breakup, and he goes to make love to her and
the camera pans over to the cigarette he's just flicked onto the bed,
slowly igniting into flames. It's as though it was designed with me in
mind as a target, in terms of the mind-fuck aspect of it, and
remember, I invited myself.) Tell him it has flashes of Tarkovsky-
esque brilliance. Use the word *nuanced*. Afterward, when he intro-
duces me to some people there as his *friend*, engage self in mental
thrashing about deeper meaning of ongoing *friend* usage (because
we may not be dating, but we're definitely not friends, and as far as
I'm concerned, when an introduction kind of scenario comes up
before you've established what you are to each other, there should
be no title or modifier of any kind). Tell him my movie's being
released nationally the following weekend. He said he can't wait to
see it and that he'll call as soon as he does.

Later that evening: Review entire evening as filmstrip pro-
jected onto bedroom curtains starring Benicio Del Toro as M. and
Christina Applegate as me.

CHRISTINA APPLEGATE: What did you mean by calling me your friend?

BENICIO DEL TORO: I meant I want to fuck you up against these curtains so that your yuppie neighbors and their purebred dogs can see the silhouettes of our writhing figures and envy our fame and spontaneous lovemaking.

CUT TO:

ARTY MONTAGE of Christina Applegate and Benicio Del Toro doing it up against the curtains, the silhouettes of them doing it up against the curtains, doing it one more time up against the curtains.

CUT TO:

YUPPIE NEIGHBOR #1 *(staring at window, holding Weimaraner on leash)*: I envy their fame.

YUPPIE NEIGHBOR #2 *(staring at window, holding Jack Russell on leash)*: I envy their spontaneous lovemaking.

CUT TO:

BENICIO DEL TORO: Goodbye, my friend Christina Applegate.

CHRISTINA APPLEGATE: Benicio Del Toro, why are you leaving?

BENICIO DEL TORO: I will leave you to always wonder about that.

ROLL CREDITS.

Make note that my fantasy sequences are still going horribly wrong.

Day 16: Unplug all phones due to national release of the film and thus the reviews, sticking with commitment to not read them even though the early buzz has been largely positive. (I just think that if I'm supposed to believe the ones that say the Congressional

Medal of Honor would not be enough to convey the significance of my contribution to contemporary cinema then I also have to believe the ones that suggest I should be permanently exiled to another planet, but not one of the good ones, like Neptune probably, and minus any reviews at all, I think I have my head on straight about the level of my talent as being better than some/ worse than others/not a genius/not an idiot; I could be quite susceptible to believing I was a genius, I think, if it was unanimously agreed, but then let's say that even one critic out of a hundred says I'm an idiot, I am just as likely to focus on the one who says I'm an idiot, and eventually come to see that I am an idiot, and overall it seems like a lose-lose situation I might just as well steer clear of.) Listen to a few good CDs and experience brief moment of unwavering belief that Owen Wilson will star in my next film, fall madly in love with me, and impregnate me with little Wilson-Byerses who will grow up and take advantage of nepotism and resent us both for it.

Day 21: Plug phones back in. Erase any and all messages that seem review-related. Receive five-minute call from M., reporting that he hasn't seen the movie yet and will see it as soon as he possibly can, but that he wants me to know that several of the people on his film had already seen it and loved it and had been discussing at length favorite scenes of theirs. (He also quotes a section of the review from the *Trib,* before I have a chance to cut him off, which is supposedly congratulatory, except it's something like "... luminous performances by the lead actresses convey a rich inner life that is not always reflected in the script," which I don't need to hear for so many reasons, not the least of which is why is he passing this on like it isn't terrible, or does he in fact see the plain and apparent terribleness of it and if so, what the fuck?) Note that in this call, exact time 5 mins. 14 secs., the word *friend* is used twice. In a five-minute call. Twice.

Day 49: Not one call since day 21. Progress from the biweekly meltdown to a constant, dull ache, a state in which the tears are held in abeyance only by a combination of exhaustion, the strength and will of my eye and throat muscles, and the avoidance of anything that might possibly bust the dike (virtually impossible as I am already prone to weeping over the evening news or even the guy who passes out flyers on Damen dressed in a hot-dog suit, which never fails to strike me as being both terribly poetic and sad but also weirdly hopeful).

Day 51: Discover fingers pressing MATTEO CELL as though separate from command of brain. Hear self inviting him to a local indie premiere, which he is unable to attend and says, *But let's definitely do something next week,* as though it's normal for fifty-one days to pass between the first date and the second. M. volunteers that he is *ashamed* that he still hasn't seen it. Immediately regret making the call. Have a small regret-based meltdown.

Day 52: Make attempts to understand and accept the simple meaning of someone not calling after a date. Delete MATTEO CELL from phone.

Day 65: Over the course of a week, exchange glances, smiles, or "hi"s with at least four different cute strangers on the street, inducing a mini-meltdown, in considering these as possible missed opportunities. As they pass by, think, Was that him? What if I never see him again? What if it's the one who smiled at me at Atomix? Or the guy from the farmer's market? Or the guy on Huron and Hoyne? What if it really is Owen Wilson? What if any one of them could have been the one, what if it's just a matter of starting an actual conversation and any one of these guys was the one and I just didn't talk to them because they were strangers? HOW DOES ANYONE MEET ANYONE IF THEY DON'T DRINK? How is it I'm only asking this question now that I've been sober for ten years?

Day 70: Meet with the other cute filmmaker to discuss a collaboration. Feel excited about the project. Carry on with life.

Day 80: Janet apologetically invites me to a party to which M. is also invited.

Day 81: Erase this information from mind until last possible minute.

Day 87: Spend party trying to act as though I just haven't gotten around to talking to M., at the other end of the table, followed by an awkward but baffling moment in which it appears that he's going to cry (in which I am thinking that I am the one who is supposed to be crying, what the hell would he have to cry about, but to which I say instead, *Are you all right?* to which he says, *I'm really sorry I didn't tell you where my head was at,* and asks if he still can, at some point, and I say yes, because I'm wondering where his head was at, and because although it seemed apparent at first glance that his head was in fact attached to his body in the normal location, it seems more apparent now that the head on his shoulders was actually some kind of duplicate replacement head and that his real head was at an undisclosed location, possibly being cleaned or borrowed or simply vacationing, and because I agree that wherever it happened to be that he should have told me where his head was at, and also because I would really like to know where his head was at, and I kind of want him to know where my head's been at, although as a friend I am always advising people to check their motives before they tell people where their head is at, primarily because I am of the belief that if you want to tell someone where your head is at with the intent of this changing them somehow, whether it be into some perfect person who understands you from that moment on or whether it's just that you want them to feel as crappy as you've been feeling, it either won't happen, which is most common if you are trying to get people to change, or it will happen, since people successfully punish people all the time for making them feel shitty, except for if this is the case, you are maybe not as highly evolved of a person as you could be, and although I have decisively concluded that this guy is not going to change into my perfect boyfriend, apparently I am somewhat interested in making him repent, and therefore, in spite of my protracted efforts at evolution over the years, not as evolved as I like to think, even though I like to think I can state things in such a way it seems that that is not my motive, and that I am tremendously straightforward and articulate about my feelings and that nothing is as big a deal as it is, for example I'll say something like *I had a great time at the beach that day, and I thought we had made a connection, and I was hurt and confused that I didn't hear from you,* which isn't entirely false, which is actually pretty much true, even if the underlying message is YOU FUCKED UP MY SUMMER).

So you know, don't try this at home. I did have one more melt-down, after I got home that night, a final meltdown in which I concluded that it would probably be best to give up, not just on this guy, which I had already done, but on all guys, because it seemed like it was the fucking hope that was fucking killing me, and it seemed like as good a solution as I'd ever come up with to just eradicate all the ruinous fucking hope. I called him the next day about getting together for a cup of coffee, and we sat down for what turned out to be several hours in which I learned of his extensive and lifelong depression, recently given new life during rehearsal for a play. The gist of it is that for his entire life he's been battling depression, largely of a self-hating nature, which I can of course relate to, although before we were finished talking I concluded that his peak levels were vastly more debilitating than mine had ever been, and that although he had been in therapy for some time and had had better and worse periods, he recently entered into a worse period again, due to unfavorably comparing himself to the other actors in his play and questioning whether his motives for wanting to be an actor at all were valid (he, unlike some of the actors I'd dated in the past, seemed at the very least to have an awareness that the adulation given to people in the performing arts, particularly famous ones, does not, ultimately, compensate for how crappy one might feel about oneself), and questioning, apparently a lifelong self-interrogation, what it really even was that he wanted to do with his life at all, which, if a thirty-six-year-old is the one asking the question, you have to real-ize is a pretty painful situation to find yourself in. I've had various careers over the years and more than a few skids off course, by and large compromises in an effort to do something more secure, thinking this would gain me the favor of certain relatives and, I don't know, society in general, but the Super 8 camera and the typewriter I got for my eighth and ninth birthdays, respectively, have always been in use, even if a lot of it was shitty, even if for years I only made movies for little birthday and Christmas presents, and even if it took some time, and a lot of people telling me I should really make longer movies, and like I said therapy, to get to the point where I a) made something decent and b) was willing to put it out into the world. The point is, I wasn't ever really wondering what I should do, it was more like will I ever do it and if so, how. I can't even imagine being his age and not having some kind of a clue. I told him I thought he wanted to be a filmmaker. He said he wasn't so sure anymore, that his experience at that festival had also caused his self-doubt to flourish, that he'd overheard someone whispering *self-indulgent* to someone else right after his film was screened, and that he punished himself by fucking his ex-girlfriend for a few weeks (the West Indian actress from the movie, big surprise), the details of which were frankly unnecessary for me to get the gist of it. He said he felt sure he wanted to do something, but truly had no idea what. Imagine. He also said that most of his friends know, and that maybe he could have mentioned to me but forgot, that when he gets like this, he tends to *check out*, meaning that he doesn't really call anyone and I guess doesn't go anywhere unless he really has to. And you know, I related to so much of what he was saying, I check out myself from time to time, but not ever when there's a cute guy out there I like, which brings me back to the notion I still couldn't get rid of, which was that this was all a big excuse.

But get this, he also told me that since we last spoke he had seen my movie six times. Six times. *All This Heavenly Glory*, briefly, is on the surface a chick flick (although the title is taken from a line in a Bruce Lee movie where the character says, *If you gaze too hard at the finger pointing to the moon, you'll miss all the heavenly glory*). It's about two lifelong best friends, each with her own profound manifestations of self-hate going on, a single mother in a difficult relationship and a painter struggling to find the courage to pursue her art, and them struggling with the envy they have about each other, the artist wishing she were in a difficult relationship as opposed to no relationship and the one in the relationship wishing she had the courage to not even be in a relationship, and the artist trying to explain that courage has nothing to do with not being in a relationship, being depressed and inherently unlovable is the reason why she's not in a relationship, and in the end neither of the characters has the typical kind of life-changing revelations you see in major motion pictures, it's more like the characters have these moments where you see some brief flashes of recognition on their faces but that still, at the end of the movie you think, Ok, well, maybe they got just a smidgen of insight but the likelihood is that these people aren't going to change radically anytime soon. It was my intent to just show people as they really are. So Matteo told me he loved the movie so much he saw it six times and all I could think to say after *Six times?* was *I wish you'd seen the movie one time and called me five times, or even one time to tell me this*, considering it had crossed my mind not a few times that he'd seen it and hated it. And he said no, that he loved it so much, and deeply related to both the characters, he related to the one unable to get out of the difficult relationship and went on at some length about his tendency to use relationships in this way, explaining that this was the first time in his entire life he'd been out of a relationship for more than six months, and that virtually every one of the women, no matter how different they seemed to the naked eye, was in some way elusive to him and that it was his life's work, more or less literally it would seem, to get these women to love him by whatever means necessary, and that the pattern was, unsurprisingly, that when they finally did fall in love with him, he couldn't bear it, and couldn't really believe it, and then would do this thing where he'd get them to break up with him so that he wouldn't have to be thought of as a bad guy after the fact, all this to illustrate one more reason he was in no position to be involved with anyone right then. He also said he related just as much to the struggling artist, because he felt like he had the soul of an artist even if he wasn't sure what kind, and he even said that he felt a certain connection to me, watching it, because even though he didn't assume it was autobiographical, he had the sense that I understood these women, which of course I do. So that was nice, even if I still was wishing he'd just called. *On the other hand,* he said, *full disclosure, I felt resentful that you'd made this brilliant film, and I have to tell you it figures into why I'm not so sure about filmmaking now, because I thought, "She's so brilliant, why would anyone like that ever want to be with me?"*

And I have to tell you I was floored when he said that, not just because it was the farthest thing from my mind that anyone would ever think such a thing, that anyone would see my movie and think of me as being better than them somehow, but also because the whole time I was working on the movie and waiting for it to come out, I'd been thinking this was going to be my ticket, that they'd be lining up outside my door, guys, that I would have infinite numbers of groupies, twenty-five-year-old, sexually charged, admiring groupies to choose from, and in that moment I couldn't really grasp that this was one very depressed and self-loathing guy saying this, and that he wasn't necessarily a spokesman for all guys, all I could think was, I'm screwed. And then it all made perfect sense, considering my whole unlovable persona, I didn't know how I couldn't have seen it before, that there was no level of cinematic brilliance I could reach, no combination of Sundance awards or Palme d'Ors or Oscars that would remedy my genetic defect. And so there I was, so stunned I wasn't sure what to say, really, and so what I said was, *The only difference between you and me is that I wrote down some observations I had and then I put it on film. I'm not brilliant.* I was trying to make him feel better, and there were parts of the statement that were true, it was essentially true, but it was also true that I was thinking that I was maybe an inch farther down the road, emotionally, if that's possible, and I'm not sure I realized it quite yet but it was the beginning of my subtle argument that he should still go out with me. So Matteo said, *I'm sure Woody Allen doesn't think he's brilliant either,* and I said, *No, I'm pretty sure Woody Allen knows he's brilliant, but it's an interesting example,* and I'm not sure he got my point but I didn't feel like explaining. Then Matteo was just back to saying how sorry he was that he hadn't told me sooner. Not a few times he said, *I know it sounds so terrible to say it's not you, and it's not personal, but it truly isn't, I'm just not in any position to get involved.* Which again gets back to my original point, which is that it's obviously way easier, if absurdly time-consuming, to fabricate involved excuses or exaggerate the relevance of existing pathologies.

And I should have been sitting there telling myself it was all for the best, and he's right, he shouldn't be involved, and I shouldn't be involved with him, the sane part of me got this but the bulk of me still wanted to get my hands into his hair and thought that if I just shook him by the shoulders and told him to get over himself, then we could get on with it, you know, together.

But then I just, okay, I lost it a little bit, because up to that point I'd been leaning back in my chair, with my whole, Hey, look how evolved and insouciant I am demeanor, sitting here talking about this, no big deal, and then I went back to my old self, and I said, *I'd bet money that you'll be in a relationship before a year is up,* guessing that this was an amount of time in which he was not going to have his career and self-hate all sewn up, and he said, *I couldn't say,* and I said, *I just think that if you were knocked out by someone none of this would make any difference,* and he said, *If I were knocked out by someone I'd run screaming in the other direction,* and since I was obviously not *someone* in this hypothetical scenario given that he didn't get up and run screaming in the other direction, and since I was increasingly having the sense that we were entering into some bizarre and hostile negotiation (which admittedly, I started), here's the worst of it, I said, *By that logic I should be exactly the kind of person you should go out with,* and he laughed and said, *Maybe, but it would have to be slow,* and I said,

I have no objection to that, and he said, *Very slow,* and even though I had really only been trying to make a point, I wasn't exactly sure what to think at that point, but I did feel like things needed to be lightened up so I said, *Well then I think you're making progress already,* and I said, *Who knows, by our year anniversary we could have gone out three, maybe four times.*

I had someplace else to be, and by then I felt I had gotten some useful information, even if I wasn't sure what I was going to do with it. We hugged goodbye, which is a whole other weird thing because it didn't seem any less meaningful than the first time, even if I had to admit it might be a different meaning. He was still talking as he walked away, so I'm not 100 percent sure what he said, but I'm almost positive the end of the sentence was *Next time.*

Charlotte Anne Has 3.4 Regrets

C HARLOTTE ANNE BYERS, age nineteen, has learned a few things about love, mostly regarding what not to do. After a late start her senior year of high school with the hopelessly smitten Eddie Greenfield, and accounting for

1) a fraction of one regret roughly equaling .4, for not giving nice-guy Greenfield more of a chance

(and which)

resulted in a slight delay of another year in between dates due to an uncertainty about whether dating was anything she had a continuing interest in, Charlotte Anne developed an all-consuming crush on junior Billy Glassmeyer (inspired entirely by his heavy-lidded green eyes and Afro of soft dark curls) in the fall of her freshman year of college. Said crush, which gained her an A in Beginning Fiction for a story that was basically copied right out of her diary at the last minute (certain names changed to "Carrie Anne Boyer" and "Benjy Grossmeyer") after a semester of being unable to satisfy her professor's desire for writing "that gave off the stench of a bleak, ugly truth" with anything genuinely fictional, also figured in significantly to an increasingly bad drinking problem. Back in New York for the summer, Charlotte Anne

makes an attempt at drying out (somewhat easier when one is living with one's parents and not out of state in a dorm next to a bar
that serves mixed drinks for a dollar), taking a job as a busgirl at
the Take One Restaurant on 56th and 10th, not coincidentally a
hangout of sorts for her stepfather, who works nearby. Charlotte
Anne quickly adopts as her overall life mentor her twenty-year-old
coworker, African American waitress Evangeline Powers. Evangeline, a dual citizen raised in Ghana who majored in drama at the
High School for Performing Arts, seems much more than only
one year older than Charlotte Anne, not because she is in any way
old looking (she is, in fact, startlingly beautiful, with dark skin,
mile-wide cheekbones, and a weirdly royal type of air about her)
but because of her obviously advanced sophistication. Charlotte
Anne likes to think she has a certain sophistication herself but
which thinking may in fact be directly offsetting whatever small
advancement of sophistication she might have over any other
teenager who went to prep school and saw a ballet. It is evident
early on from Evangeline's fantastic posture, not to mention her
habit of ending pretty much every sentence with an unseen but
unmistakable exclamation point (any sentence that doesn't end
this way is spoken entirely in italics; even if she pulls Charlotte
Anne aside to tell her *the kitchen just ran out of clam sauce,* there's always
an urgency that makes C.A. feel like she's just been let in on a vital
secret), that Evangeline is worth watching. Evangeline, currently
starring as Cordelia in *King Lear* at the Holy Redeemer Church in
Brooklyn, has *principles,* often in the form of quotes and among
them:

a) never sell out

b) to thine own self be true

c) those who dare, truly live.

Charlotte Anne is just trying to get through her shift. So compelling is Evangeline Powers that Charlotte Anne devotes long passages in her diary to possible ways of modeling herself after Evangeline, included among them dropping out of college to become an actress, which hadn't previously been of any interest but seems very exciting the way Evangeline describes it. (*I got three lines in a* Scorsese *film. . . . He phoned me* himself *and said, "It's* Marty." *Marty!*) It seems as good an idea at this point as struggling to fit in and get good grades at what Charlotte Anne knew by the end of her first semester was the wrong college and accounting for

2) one full regret; of the two schools Charlotte Anne was accepted into, University of Vermont and Mason College, C.A. easily decided upon Mason on the basis of its not being in the middle of nowhere; because she couldn't picture herself wearing Docksiders and drinking beer, she ended up wearing designer clothes she couldn't afford and drinking anything with sour mix

(but)

a plummeting grade point average made transferring somewhere else unlikely.

A temporary distraction from junior Billy Glassmeyer comes in the form of a fuzzy-haired blond bartender named Steven

Saccavino, who mixes drinks in the service bar (not much bigger than a very small closet just past the swinging doors inside the kitchen) and develops a major crush on Charlotte Anne (more accurately he falls deeply in love with her almost overnight, offering continuous displays and declarations of his ardor, making nosegays out of toothpicks and olives, stealing shy kisses on the cheek when she has her hands full of dirty dishes, and making frequent marriage proposals). Charlotte Anne, who claims to be quite ambivalent about S.S., admits (to Evangeline only) to liking the attention possibly more than mere ambivalence allows, but nonetheless will admit only that she has never met anyone quite like Saccavino and doesn't think there's any harm in just being friends. Charlotte Anne and Steven spend a good deal of time together outside of work, mostly walking around and talking for hours. Steven has a knack for asking pointed questions about her hopes and dreams that no one else seems to have much interest in, least of all Billy Glassmeyer, and drawing a variety of romantic scenarios in which he and Charlotte Anne ride off happily into the sunset, which serves both to enchant her and to leave her seriously disturbed. C.A. Byers alternates between wondering whether she should kiss him or whether he has some very severe mental problems that she cannot avoid noticing, as she has never met anyone with quite such a colorful past, certainly not anyone who is twenty years old, although he appears to be 100 percent sincere both in his feelings for her and in the telling of his life story, which includes one about having sex with a woman three times his age (considering the mathematical angle here, at any combination of ages, the gap is always going to be discomforting), which he refers to as the loss of his virginity, which Charlotte Anne thinks isn't a phrase anyone can reasonably use when the younger party is *ten*, and which, along with many of his stories, she will have cause, against her will, to picture in her head repeatedly. Charlotte Anne finds these stories to be so horrifying and tragic that she has reason to believe he is making them all up, even though he isn't. Over the course of the summer, Steven Saccavino tells many more stories, including that he occasionally took money for sexual favors from the time he lost his virginity until he was about fifteen, insisting that he didn't think of it as prostitution but that it was in some way pleasurable for him and that any monies received were always a sort of afterthought, like a little thank-you; that when he first moved to New York he lived briefly at the 79th Street Boat Basin (not in a boat, but in the underpass); that he and his roommate Hank have only one bed and that they both coincidentally sleep in the nude, all of which, it should also be said, are told in such a way, because of a general demeanor of innocence, that it appears that the more shocking aspects of the tales are almost always not the main point of the story, as if, for example, he was telling the story of his first ice-cream cone and then just happened to lose his virginity to the thirty-year-old who bought it for him. Charlotte Anne makes many entries in her journal of a should-I-shouldn't-I nature, arguments swaying her toward the shouldn't-I side including her stepfather's readily apparent dislike of Saccavino (almost always backed up by the question, "Whatever happened to That Nice Eddie?") for reasons she's never certain of except for that he considers Steven to be "spacey" and says that she could "do better" and accounting for

3) another almost 1.6 regrets; many years later, Charlotte Anne will wonder not a little and not infrequently if she really could have done better; though the evidence is initially strongly against him, Steven Saccavino will go on to build a successful contracting business from scratch, and marry and produce two beautiful fuzzy-headed children.

(Not to mention)

that he was madly in love with Charlotte Anne in a way no one really has been at this point. (Okay, well, Eddie Greenfield was kind of in love with her too, but wasn't quite so dramatic about it. And Chuck Farley with the one testicle [never seen by C.A. but frequently spoken about by others] who liked her an awful lot. Later there would also be that guy with the office job who said she was everything he'd ever dreamed of, but his right-wing politics and chewed fingernails would pretty quickly get in the way. And she never really counted Brad the flower-bearing *Star Search*™ winner or Mike the letter-writing ornithologist [he wore sandals], because they barely even got in the door. And then there was the film director who flew her to Maine for a lobster dinner, and also the advertising guy who made her laugh a lot but bore a strong resemblance to Art Garfunkel. Plus also her slightly overweight next-door neighbor who left homemade pies on her doormat [rejected more on the basis of his lumberjack-type looks than his being slightly overweight].) By the time she goes back to college it briefly ends up turning into a should-I-have discourse on the basis of a series of misspelled love letters from Saccavino that say things like "if you'r busy I could easily sit with a glass wine and watch you think for few huors" and "when you come home we can walk around the Village a litle drunk while it snows only on us my love." Charlotte Anne has never gotten anything remotely resembling a love letter and thinks this is more romantic even than the rare copy of Billy Joel's *Cold Spring Harbor* that Eddie Greenfield had given her the day before she broke up with him, but due in equal parts to Steven's intense feelings and the misspellings/missing prepositions and articles (although she is consistently charmed by the self-portrait always accompanying his signature, a slightly distorted smiley face with one wayward curl sprouting from the top of his head), Charlotte Anne abruptly stops answering his letters, and by this time she has already lost her virginity anyway, to Billy Glassmeyer after a drunken Saturday night at a gay disco, and accounting for

4) another approximately .4. Charlotte Anne didn't so much regret the loss as she did her choice of Billy Glassmeyer, not a shining moment; the then senior, having had what must have been considerable (at least by comparison to Charlotte Anne) sexual experience, felt the need to share all the fruits of that experience with Charlotte Anne in that one evening (proving what, she had no idea, although she was certain he was aiming for something), which amounted to a marathon of sorts that C.A. would thankfully not ever re-create, even

after gaining some experience/renewed interest in the area. (Undoubtedly it does figure in that Billy was a big-time pothead, and that his duration in this instance may have had something to do with being on a lot of drugs.)

Charlotte Anne also gets several letters from Evangeline, reporting on this or that love affair and saying that Steven Saccavino walks around like a zombie without her, brokenhearted at the news of the Billy Glassmeyer fiasco. Evangeline's letters, always signed off "to thine own self be true," account for

5) another full regret, as it would be quite some time before Charlotte Anne figured out

    a) what that even meant

and

    b) a way to do it.

Home for Christmas break, Charlotte Anne runs into Evangeline Powers in front of O'Neal's Balloon, where Evangeline excitedly makes note of the *serendipity* of the moment as she is only in New York for two days before flying back to L.A. to finish a sitcom pilot she describes as *What's Happenin'* meets *Three's Company!* E.P. adds that she hasn't heard anything from Saccavino for a while, which is definitely a disappointment, but Charlotte Anne is still back on *sitcom pilot*, trying to figure out how this aligns itself with any of Evangeline's principles and concluding that it seems an obvious conflict with both principles one and two and although three is up for debate, considering the formulaic aspect of the TV project in question, Charlotte Anne decides that it doesn't seem daring at all, that it seems like the opposite. Combined disappointments aside,

Charlotte Anne feels marginally pleased with herself for recognizing the compromised principles at all, and immediately decides to employ principle number three (ruling out numbers one and two on the basis of her not having established what she might possibly have to sell out at this point and also due to her still not knowing what the hell two means) by impulsively purchasing a bunch of daisies from the closest Korean market and hopping a cab to the Upper East Side in the hopes of some kind of epiphany/romantic reunion with Steven Saccavino. Charlotte Anne pushes the buzzer that says SACCAVINO but the voice that answers is decidedly older and crankier and possibly Chinese, and although she has a pretty strong feeling she missed the boat, asks if Steven is home. The older, crankier, possibly Chinese voice says, "No live here now," and Charlotte Anne, disappointed again but

6) subtracting a full regret on account of the attempted implementation of E. Powers's principle number three,

goes home to put the flowers in a vase.

Guidelines

START THE DAY as usual like this:

Say *fuck* when the alarm goes off even though it's a more or less perfect fall day, understanding that this daily *fuck* is three parts habit from when you used to have to actually be somewhere/one part reaction to extreme unpleasantness of the alarm. Compensate by muttering the serenity prayer before you toss back the covers. Make coffee, prepare Froot Loops to correct degree of sogginess (moderate), check e-mail, "watch" *Today* show, attempt *Times* crossword (it's Tuesday, so be sure to congratulate self on your Mon.–Wed. genius level), "read" rest of paper (quote marks indicating actual participation in these particular activities). Check back page for obituaries. No one under eighty. No need to check to see how they died to reconfirm belief that cancer and god have personalities and that they are in some sort of pact that involves taking what you think is an unreasonable percentage of good under-eighty-year-old people for reasons that don't get explained in the obituaries. Finish turning pages of *Times* in cool breeze on porch, smell/prune/admire/appreciate flowers, appreciate porch/*Times*/cool breeze/hazelnut coffee/not having to be anywhere, relax (as much as that is possible, with you being you in spite of the not having to be anywhere) via distant sound of trains/church bells/close and loud sound of birds chirping, if anyone asks plan to refer to all this as "meditation." Receive daily morning call from Jenna, reporting about the latest disaster with her pernicious, narcissistic, unclean boyfriend. Come to believe in evil via the p/n/u boyfriend, who has surpassed limits of asshole you previously thought impossible. Long past the point where you have any compassion for the hardships (however extreme) that led him to this condition, long past the point where you started telling Jenna once a day to dump his fucked-up ass (policy generally being to avoid this kind of hard-and-fast advice given your sense that friends tend to dump the friend telling them to dump their boyfriend and not the boyfriend), you endure daily revelations of his pernicious, narcissistic uncleanlinesss today, including a stunning description of p/n/u's apartment (he has photos of himself all over the apartment, mostly photos that don't include anyone else, and when you say, *Oh my god*, Jenna says, *And they're three-deep*), culminating in this morning's argument in which he compared your best friend to a kind of cancer. Think *cunt* would be nicer than *cancer*. Feel something close to hate. Think about praying for him. Hold off, wondering if he deserves it.

Check e-mail again, glance at TV, think, *Something has gone horribly wrong at air traffic control.* Thirty minutes later, recognize this as one of your last innocent thoughts, which is ironic considering you thought you had your last one twenty years ago (something along the lines of *My grandparents lived to be a hundred, therefore my parents will never die*). Fail to ever get a complete grasp on what just happened. Leave TV on for a week straight (a lot even for you), read every word of everything on the subject in your sight for the following year just in case enlightenment follows.

Fail to reach Jenna, your stepdad, your cousin, your stepbrother Chris in D.C., a dozen other friends. Call Dad even though he lives in Iowa. Try e-mail. One way or another, by the end of the day, get through to/get word of the safety of everyone you're close to who still lives back east. Feel as though you abandoned New York/as though New York has a personality and that it has just been wounded very badly/that you should have been there/that this wouldn't have happened if you hadn't abandoned New York/guilty for having previously thought that it was New York who abandoned you and spit you out like a bad grape. Feel relief/horror/despair/gratitude/dread simultaneously. Wish for one day/afternoon/hour in your entire life with only a single emotion, preferably one of the good ones.

And then this:

Jenna calls to say that the Dans are missing. You haven't seen the Dans in fifteen years, but it's neither here nor there. Dan Parker worked on the 103rd floor. Dan Julian was at Windows on the World. Maintain belief/denial for nine days that people will be found, try to think of any good reason why Dan P.'s family would go ahead and have a memorial service on the seventh day when there are surely hundreds or thousands of people alive and well in a giant air pocket in the basement living perfectly well on Jamba Juice and Cinnabons.

Remember this:

You and your best friend Jenna Ritter are twenty-one. Actually you're twenty-one; Jenna will remind you for the rest of your life that she's four months younger and at this time, only twenty. Explain repeatedly that this does not make her a year younger four months out of the year, even when she tells you *Shut up.* You are a guest at the Ritters' house in Seaview for the summer, working as a cocktail waitress at McDonough's restaurant in *town* (aka Ocean Beach, the next community over).

Do this every day: Put on purple striped bikini. Eat cereal. Go to beach. Walk several miles in both directions. Swim. Read. Achieve unprecedented Coppertone tan. Hang with lifeguards. Develop severe crush on tall blond but somewhat silent Dan P. Flirt with less silent Tico and Jack and Gary and Donnie and Dan J. but rebuff any serious advances from any of the above even though Jack tries to insist you need mouth-to-mouth *preventively* and Dan J. calls you *legitimately gorgeous* and despite the fact that for several summers you've had a separate but milder crush on Dan P.'s friend Donnie who says things like *the caliber of that bikini, and the wearer thereof, is high.* Leave beach only for *Days of Our Lives,* lunch (turkey sandwiches on a poppy-seed roll with lettuce, tomato, and too much salt), recap of current crushes with Jenna (recently extricated from intense five days with Gary, currently hot and heavy with Dan P.'s college friend Andy). Understand that on Fire Island there are certain unwritten laws to maximize Fire Island experience:

1.   Wardrobe must be limited to: One bathing suit. One outfit/uniform, preferably something well-worn, modified only by addition of a light jacket in the event of

rain or a cooler evening. Come to know people simply by what they wear (e.g., neighbor in polo shirt down the street known only as Pink Man). This summer, your outfit is a Fiorucci jean miniskirt and a well-worn work shirt with a tank top underneath. Jenna's is a pair of carpenter pants *(carps)* with the well-worn white Stones t-shirt you gave her that belonged to one of your exes that you'd rather not be reminded of every single day except she won't leave the house in anything else. (She'll try, there is a ritual of trying, a more or less daily ritual of trying that involves a series of well-worn t-shirts of her own, but they are always abandoned after a very long hour in which you are required to be present for some sort of advising that never takes hold, in favor of the original Stones tee. Additionally you will be required to stand by in a similar way with relation to Jenna's hair, which is almost always a pointless exercise given the inevitability of "Fire Island hair" [some mutation of unseeming size/frizz setting in almost as soon as you set foot outdoors].)

2. Do not attempt to stay friends/keep in touch with more than one person from F.I. per *winter* (aka, all seasons that aren't summer) *off the island*, but use this person to keep apprised of everyone's whereabouts and well-being. Do this for the rest of your lives.

3. Try to understand that as far as dating goes, it is extremely casual, even if you think it's serious, and that there will be overlap insofar as over the years you and Jenna will end up being able to say that you made out with four of the same

guys, whether you wanted to or not. You have already
both made out with Jack and agree that he kisses like a
bird. (Gain unfortunate knowledge later that Jack's
brother Chase also kisses like a bird, leading to a long
discussion with Jenna about the basis of the birdlike
kissing given that neither you nor Jenna has ever kissed a
bird, and whether or not kissing styles are genetic, or
whether it has something to do with the shape of the
tongue, if the birdlike tongue prevented any hope of non-
birdlike kissing or whether retraining would be possible
[if you were interested, which you were not, based on
their personalities — you will end up kissing Jack one
more time ten years in the future at which time he will tell
you he needs you more *as a friend* to which you say, *We
haven't been in touch in ten years,* to which he says, *Okay then let's
keep making out,* at which time you remember rule #2].) If
possible, avoid overlapping in same summer. (Do not
attempt overlapping off the island. Learn this by
attempting to overlap off the island when Jenna comes to
visit you at college and sleeps with the guy you had a
secret crush on for two years, on the technicality that you
tried to fix them up in the first place, not to mention that
she didn't really know about the crush. Make this worse
before you graduate by sleeping with him yourself under
the worst but hardly unusual sort of circumstances in
which you are both very drunk and you are the third
person he's asked to go home with him when the bar
closes, all of this resulting in two fights with Jenna about

how *she should have known* [your expectation of Jenna's mind-reading capabilities having fully set in right around this time and mostly having to do with *considering your feelings* (not realizing until long into the future that she's often been way better at this than you)], followed also by never speaking to the guy again starting the morning after. Forget this experience entirely but learn it for good six years later after she fixes you up with the guy she eventually ends up marrying [who you found to be incredibly inconsiderate of your many feelings]. Make sure this leads to near destruction of the friendship so that lesson-learning is complete.)

4. Find yourself unable to ever re-create the F.I. experience anywhere else and if you're a *native*, return to F.I. every year and stay with your parents until you have children of your own and then keep returning with your children. If you're a *moocher*, move away from New York and always wish there were anyplace else like Fire Island anywhere much less within a few hours of Chicago, which there isn't. Wonder if you could be some sort of reverse Robert Moses somewhere and replace roads with sidewalks and get all the old gang to buy houses there and start all over again. Obviously not.

Do this every night: Drink one or two free pitchers of frozen banana daiquiris after work (always waking up the next morning without a hangover because you are twenty-one and thus giving you one more thing to add to the list of things that feed your denial for another nine years, e.g., you don't drink every day/never missed a day of work/always remember to pull your hair back when you throw up/get the notes from someone else after you sleep through class/never had an accident [never mind that you don't have a license and therefore don't drive]/stopped adding downers to your alcohol after the Karen Ann Quinlan thing) and head to the Alligator to meet Jenna and dance with Tico and Donnie and Dan J. and Dan P. Tico and Dan J. admire your moves and make you feel ready to call up Denney Terrio/Don Cornelius and boogie down on syndicated TV. Dan P. doesn't dance and looks uncomfortable just watching people dance but you imagine he is silently aroused by your advanced disco. Struggle for conversation (e.g., *Are you excited about going to Europe? Totally,* nod a lot), but feel the love when he buys you a beer. Do this every night until Labor Day weekend, then walk home with him on the beach after a beer bash and make out by the dunes. Enjoy this on many levels excepting Dan P.'s two-day beard and ask if maybe he could shave the next time. Report back to Jenna that you and Dan P. *French-kissed.* Jenna reports to you that Donnie and Dan J. both have crushes on you, wonder if it would be a conflict to date/French-kiss all of them. Ask Jenna why so many guys have crushes on you on Fire Island but not off the island. Jenna explains that on Fire Island the crushes are rampant/overt/in constant rotation but also that chances are there are just as many guys who like you off the island and you just don't know about it. (Find this suspect at best in spite of Jenna's sincere and indestructible optimism.) Do this the next day: Pretend like you're cool. Make much out of the fact that Dan P. shaved the next day even though there's suddenly not much to talk about and you will never French-kiss him again. Make much out of the one postcard you get from Dan P. during his semester abroad that says *See you soon.* Read an encyclopedia of his unspoken feelings in between *See* and *you* and *soon.* Under the influence of alcohol, try to forget Dan P. by sleeping with your fucking buddy who's also everyone else's fucking buddy. Swear off men and alcohol until Dan P. gets back from overseas until three weeks later, and then, under the influence of alcohol, try to forget Dan P. by sleeping with your fucking buddy who's also everyone else's fucking buddy. Graduate college. Go to one F.I. reunion party in the city a few years later and remember how cute Dan P. was when he tells you you look great and say to each other, *We should do something soon,* but then never see or speak to him again.

Snap back to:

Jenna's report on the memorial service, how many people were there, how Fire Island will never be the same. Tell her you love her, expecting her to say *Cut it out* even though she tells you she loves you too. Realize the number of times you or Jenna have said this to each other since seventh grade might add up to the fingers on one hand, that this may be the only area where either of you are in touch with your masculine side, in your belief that the hug is overrated, that it is your right as New Yorkers to decline any unwarranted hugging, which you believe there is a lot of. Realize you might be wrong.

Discover a week later that Jenna had had another fight with the pernicious, narcissistic, unclean boyfriend regarding her behavior the morning of the 11th in which she rushed to her son's school to pick him up before thinking to call p/n/u to say there was a change of plans, in which p/n/u noted that her ex-husband was lucky to have dumped her inconsiderate ass (which was um, more or less extremely the opposite of what happened) and condemned not just Jenna but *all mothers worldwide* as being evil and unkind (Jenna Ritter being hardly perfect but about as far from evil or unkind as is possible — you've always said that the difference between you and Jenna is that Jenna's nicer, that she's not the kind of girl who says *fuck* in the morning, even though she has plenty of reasons to right now, even though she's had plenty of reasons to before, even though you've sometimes been the reason, e.g., when you skipped her wedding because you took it personally that she married someone who was inconsiderate of your feelings, she's the kind of girl who says *yay* in the morning, and has plenty of reasons to, starting with her awesome ten-year-old who took one look at p/n/u before the abuse set in and said, *He seems like a nice guy but I think he has a lot of anger inside him*), and although Jenna is willing to concede that she wasn't necessarily thinking straight on that particular morning, agree with her that under the circumstances she deserves understanding. The city exploded. A mom went to get her kid. Somehow, a guy took this personally. Start a letter to p/n/u using adverbs like *extremely* and *utterly* and *absurdly* to modify words like *sinister* and *self-obsessed* and *vituperative* but realize your anger may be somewhat misdirected six pages later when you get to *evildoer*. Pray for him instead. Fly home six weeks later. Survey the gate for people who might be willing to kick ass on an as-needed basis. Make note of most silent moment you've ever experienced when the skyline, or absence of it, comes into view. Forgive your stepfather for remarrying. Go back to being exactly the same as before, only different.

✦

The Evolution of the Thing

✦

LUCY LOUISE MILLER, age four and a half, reminds Charlotte of herself at that age, if she had any early childhood memories, which she doesn't. (Charlotte Byers has been told that she was a talkative, tree-climbing, knee-skinning two-to-five-year-old, but life for Charlotte began, for better or worse, in New York City at age six as a shy only child with a southern accent and a bowl haircut.) She is greeted warmly at the door to the Millers' house by Lucy's parents, Jane and Scratch (there has been an explanation for this name that is less than appetizing, but the truth is that Scratch is a gentle, baby-faced young dad), and Lucy, who has been anticipating Charlotte and her boyfriend Colin's arrival for days, says, *Hey, um, Charlotte? Hey what's up I'm Lucy and this is a sign on my door that says my name L-U-C-Y and that's a heart next to it it's a red heart red is my favorite color do you want to see my room okay come on look it's purple and has polka dots.* Jane and Scratch joke that they'll see Charlotte on her way out, knowing that once Lucy has attached herself to someone there's little chance she'll pry herself off unless there's a Wallace and Gromit movie involved. Charlotte tells Lucy that her room is purple too but there are no polka dots, and Lucy tells her she should get her boyfriend Colin to paint her some.

It's July fourth weekend. Charlotte and her boyfriend Colin are in his hometown of Kalamazoo.

Some of the ways in which this is new:

1. Charlotte has never gone home with a boyfriend before.
2. Charlotte has never used the word *boyfriend* before, without irony.
3. Charlotte has a boyfriend.

Scratch is one of a wide circle of Colin's oldest friends. He and Jane, preparing a barbecue at their modest home (outfitted with ten-dollar sofas that Charlotte wishes existed in Chicago and an equally enviable art collection made mostly by Scratch or their friends), are, Charlotte observes, as much Colin's family now as his own family. Charlotte has met Jane and Scratch once before, in Chicago. It went well. (She could have met them the first week she and Colin were dating, but she heard *friends* and *punk show* and passed on the invitation, picturing dudes and beer and pogoing instead of the easygoing parents of a four-year-old.) Colin has been to New York with Charlotte and met her best friend Jenna and hung with Jenna and her son and he met her stepfather and they had lunch and it went well. In another week they will go to Iowa where he will meet her father and possibly some assorted siblings and she is not even worried a little about if it will go well.

One way in which this is not new:

1. Colin is younger.
2. By a lot.

3. It's not creepy or anything, it's just a lot. We don't need to
   say how much.
4. Except that there have been younger. So there's that.

Somewhere along the line Charlotte very unintentionally
started dating younger guys until it became a thing, even though
she will still insist that it's not a preference sort of thing but just a
who-she-meets sort of thing (and if she ever had a real thing, it
could be easily argued that it was a non-age-specific, emotionally
unavailable type thing, which type thing, she has discovered through
a great deal of trial and error, or maybe error and error is a better
way to put it, is an all-ages show). Prior to turning thirty she had
dated older guys and younger guys and same-age guys just to point
out that there exists statistical evidence of her having no particular
preference. That said, she has theories about the evolution of the
alleged thing. The brief mission statement of the evolution of the
thing is that she has in a way aged backward, but in a good way.
Charlotte Anne Byers, born at age six in New York City with a bad
haircut to a hyper/ambitious/loving/weepy mom and a missing
dad (Charlotte deduced some decades later that there must have
been an explanation involving the words *divorce* and *Iowa* that took
place sometime before her memory loss), arguably fits an earlier
theory quite well, one held by her stepfather's deceased father, who
hypothesized that everyone is born a certain age and stays that age.
His favorite example was that his son was born forty, and this
would bear itself out quite well over the years; he is who he is,
always, a man with none of the apparent or even subtle discomfort
that pretty much applies in one way or another to every single

other person Charlotte has ever met, an extremely straightforward, personable, and funny but responsible young man who at twenty-nine married an older woman (Charlotte's mother) and at fifty-nine married a younger woman (Charlotte's stepfather's new wife, which is admittedly beyond clunky, but, you know, welcome to the twenty-first century). Charlotte might use Lucy Louise Miller as a case study, as she appears to have been born at age twenty-five, with equal interests in Björk and *Finding Nemo.* At age six, Charlotte Anne Byers had a rich internal life but remained reserved and shy until about her freshman year of college when alcohol became available, and starting around age twelve, she was frequently mistaken for older until somewhere around twenty-one, when suddenly and overnight the opposite became true, which was sort of annoying at the time but which she would eventually be pretty obviously grateful for. At thirty she would quit drinking and begin, slowly, absurdly, painfully so, to turn her life around, including and not insignificantly somehow learning to be comfortable in the world, or more comfortable would be more accurate, she has more or less traded in the goal of ever reaching some perfect comfort level for the new and more realistic goal of being just a little more comfortable than she is at any given point or as an offshoot of this, being willing to accept that her comfort level is not what she'd like, therefore theoretically affording her some comfort to the extent that she'll sometimes give herself five minutes off from wishing she were at the next comfort level up. It helps not a little that she's finally found a world she's more comfortable in, which turns out not to be the world she'd been in since she was six, which probably seemed obvious all along to everyone except Charlotte, but you try leaving New York if that's where you're from, it's problematic. Also and plus it would take her until her late thirties to make a career for herself out of something she actually wanted to do and plus also, at forty, she still passes for thirty (if you squint, she'll say) and doesn't dress her age particularly, she's not going around like Britney or anything, but added a couple of tattoos and mixes some vintage in there and so she meets guys who, she guesses, just don't immediately know. Not that she would ever lie, she wouldn't, but that's who she meets. But she will argue that it is not a preference and can make a pretty good and obvious case for why it might be a lot easier with someone closer to her own age. But it didn't happen, and so here comes the very adorable shaggy-haired Colin who seems not to care about the age difference and makes crazy beautiful bookshelves and paints and draws and who loves old buildings and *This American Life* and tapes stuff for her dad who he's never even met and gives her a Yo La Tengo record with love songs on it and says, *This makes me think of you*, and treats her well and is sweet and smart and funny and easy to be around, is the main thing, she feels as though she can really be herself around him which is sort of the opposite of how she's felt with almost everyone she's ever dated, with whom she felt she should actually be someone else (and always had the impossible task of trying to figure out who she should be but who was usually someone who could name all the members of the cabinet and looked like Angelina Jolie). So Colin, some years younger, is very cool, and he's a carpenter, he *carpents*, as Jenna says, and he's an artist, and his friends are all artists of one kind or another, and this is a universe Charlotte's been in and around since she moved to Chicago and also has a lot of feelings about but wonders sometimes where this universe was in New York because she sort of got stuck on the Upper West Side long after the artiness of it had morphed into trader and stroller world and so anyway Charlotte looks at her Chicago friends and Colin's Kalamazoo friends and it occurs to her that there was some confusion about the date of her birth with the dude in charge insofar as it seems to have been approximately ten years too soon and actually wonders if you could legally change your birth date in the same way some people change their names, if you could argue, *You know, 1972 just feels more* me. So what happens is she feels simultaneously more comfortable in this world than any other world while also being kind of peripherally aware that she is forty and they aren't. But it's fine and the main thing is that she believes that Colin has considered the issue and, while also being aware that she is forty and he isn't, believes that love is love and also that Charlotte is kind of hot, and also it's kind of been acknowledged more or less without even needing to have too much discussion about it that the collective loss/illness factor between them is on the high side, point being that you just never know. What's sort of interesting is that in New York, Colin, who has some discomforts of his own, social and otherwise, fared surprisingly well the entire weekend, even at a party where he knew no one besides Charlotte, had arguably been as relaxed as Charlotte has ever seen him (this being a rare sentence in which the words *Charlotte* and *relaxed* and *New York* will appear together, as her New York—related stress has only increased since her departure), while in Kalamazoo a parallel will occur in which Charlotte, who might have reasonable cause to feel uncomfortable with Colin's friends that she barely knows, feels as relaxed and calm as is possible for her to be, while Colin kind of freaks out inside a little bit from a similar sort of stimulation, a too-much-backstory kind of sensory overload that Charlotte has in New York (minus a few million people).

After dinner Scratch's mom meets up with everyone on the front porch for some pre-fireworks fireworks (some brought in by Colin fresh from a giant warehouse in Indiana that sells only fireworks, not even a gum ball, only fireworks, and they have shopping carts and they have crowds and the shopping carts are full and Colin is super psyched and given that he is not the athletic type but more of the arty introspective type, he does not also seem like the firework type except that he is also a Midwestern boy and around these parts of the Midwest anyway, everyone, Charlotte learns, is the firework type) and Colin and Charlotte give Lucy a package of B'loonies (a knockoff of Super Elastic Bubble Plastic, weird-smelling soft plastic in a tube you blow up into balloon-like shapes with a straw), an impulse buy at the BP made as much for the purposes of Charlotte re-creating the good parts of her childhood as it is for Lucy's fun. Lucy takes it upon herself to introduce Charlotte to her grandmother, saying, *Grandma this is Colin's girlfriend Charlotte,* moments later introducing her to the neighbors as *Colin's girlfriend Charlotte* to everyone's amusement and when Jane suggests to Lucy that she can whittle that down to just Charlotte, Charlotte says it's fine and explains that even though she's been given license to freely use the term, she uses it sparingly but secretly enjoys hearing it out loud as often as possible. The artists blow up the B'loonies and manage to put them together into something that looks like it could actually go into a museum, which Scratch photographs and Jane subsequently titles *Not a Gum*, from a warning on the package, to which Charlotte adds, *B'loonies/Digital Image, Collaboration, 2003.* Which will be one of a growing list of repeated jokes for the weekend that will include but not be limited to things known as

1. Colin's Stomach.
2. Shine!
3. Jefferson Starship.
4. Setting on fireworks. (As opposed to setting them *off*, which makes no sense in the mind of one Lucy Louise Miller.)

The rest of which will be explained soon enough, but mentioning numbers one and three are relevant insofar as Colin has been asking Charlotte to write something about him in which he's a really funny guy, which is hard both because what's funny about Colin tends to be sort of subtle and not easily translatable to the screenplay format necessarily but also because of the lack of conflict thing, which tends to help any compelling stories, Charlotte feels. The stomach thing had come about during dinner when Charlotte noticed that Colin's shirt was buttoned somewhat haphazardly so that the top button and the bottom buttons were buttoned but not the center buttons, leaving his somewhat hairy middle exposed, which became even more amusing when Colin thought to participate in the Millers' wig-and-giant-glasses photo series by putting the giant glasses into his stomach and a cigarette in his navel, resulting in an alarmingly lifelike human face, albeit one that somewhat resembled a satanic and boozy Cabbage Patch doll. Joke number three refers to Colin's sudden songwriting inspiration in which a record cover is transformed into, for better or worse, an unforgettable tune called "Jefferson Starship." Which goes, *Jefferson Staaarship. Jefferson Star-ship. Jefferson Staaarship. Jefferson Star-ship. Jefferson Starship.* Okay, whatever, but just know that there is a lot of laughter over the weekend.

So but there is one incident over the weekend, the incident at the cliff, Charlotte will call it, even though it would be more appropriate to call it the incident at the dune, since it is a dune and not a cliff, even though it seems extremely cliff-like from the perspective of Charlotte looking down from the top of the dune/cliff, it looks to her kind of like a straight drop, anyway at the bottom of the dune/cliff is a secluded beach, and somehow after getting out of the car, Charlotte and Colin lag behind the Miller family and their friends Matt and his son, also known as Lucy's boyfriend/husband Oliver (originator of Shine!, which he learned in music class, which is basically like jazz hands except you have to also say, *Shine!*), who are down the dune and/or cliff combination, out of their clothes and into the water before Colin and Charlotte even reach the edge, at which time Charlotte pretty much freaks at the height and cannot imagine how she might make it down, and as moments pass and Colin tries to reassure her that it's no big deal, goes through a progression in her head whereby everyone present (including the dread-headed stoners around a bonfire who she doesn't even know) has reversed their existing positive opinions of her into something along the lines of, *Wow she's so old she's from like prehistoric times and who is she kidding with those tattoos we were so totally wrong about her did you notice she didn't take her jewelry off and how much makeup she's wearing can you even believe she wore makeup and jewelry to the beach you know her movies aren't all that and wow we've never met anyone so lame,* but expanded considerably into something of a mental dissertation. (One of Charlotte's few insecurities about her looks is the sad state of her complexion, and she has perfected a non-makeup makeup over the years, but Colin will come close to convincing her she looks better without it, close enough to get her to lose the mascara, anyway, and actually her complexion has seen a noticeable improvement since she started seeing Colin; as he says, *The lovin' helps.*) Colin tries to explain to Charlotte how to walk down a dune, which makes sense in the telling but not in her body, and she tries to explain that she is trying not to cry and feels like a big loser, and he tells her it's okay if she wants to cry or even if she doesn't want to go down and she says she has to go down and he says she really doesn't and tells her he loves her and she says she's a loser and he says she's not a loser and he hugs her a bunch of times and somehow she gets down the dune and into the water just in time for the sun to go under followed by thunderstorms twenty minutes later (climbing up the dune, particularly under the threat of lightning, will not be nearly the same kind of obstacle as the descent) and at no time will there be any actual evidence that even a passing comment about Charlotte not going down the dune has been made.

Things Charlotte Writes Down in Her Journal Pretty Much Every Time Colin Says Them

1. *I love you*
2. *I missed you so much* (especially if he'd last seen her, like, the day before)

3. *I can't wait to see you* (especially if he'd last seen her, like, the
    day before)

4. Assorted and miscellaneous compliments often involving
    the words *hot* and *foxy* because the thing is that Colin is
    really the first person to ever say number one unless you
    count Steven Saccavino, who she didn't really even date
    and certainly didn't kiss and which was twenty years ago,
    and so you can imagine why she might want to write that
    down every time until she doesn't feel like writing it down
    anymore, because of the waiting, and plus it seems
    particularly great, better than she could have imagined
    because he always says it at really great times, times when
    she needs to hear it and times when it seems unexpected
    but never without meaning, always with lots of meaning,
    and so the point is that Charlotte Anne Byers is in love
    with someone who is also in love with her, and says so
    with meaning, even though it turns out that being in love
    with someone who loves you and says so with meaning
    doesn't mean you're not still you and you being Charlotte
    Anne/Charlie/Charlotte Byers means that even if you
    have a couple of tattoos and make cool movies and can
    stand to be around people a little better than you could
    before you reverse-aged, you still spin in your head about
    stuff sometimes and so might your boyfriend, and that
    even though it is apparently not in and of itself a
    problem solver, the love, that said, it's pretty sweet, and
    she'll take it.

Football

IN MY NEXT LIFE I want to explain homecoming to someone, enthusiastically. I want to understand what it means to say that something is the size of a football field and I want an older brother named Jimmy who plays tight end and I want to know the names of all the players and I want them to carry me over their heads to the bus and I want to eat pizza with them after the game. I want to go to all the home games and all the away games and wear blue eyeliner and use Sun-In and I want to make out under the bleachers and I want to wear the halfback's jacket. I want to squint in the bright lights and bring a thick plaid blanket and something hot in a thermos and I want to see my breath as I scream Rah or Whoo or Go team for the Tigers or the Hawks or the Wildcats. I want Jimmy to get a football scholarship to State and I want to call my dad Pop and I want to beg Pop to lend me his pickup to drive downstate to my brother's games and when Jimmy gets suspended from the team for being involved in an "incident" with a coed and swears he wasn't involved in the incident I want to believe him and when he drives his car into a telephone pole at ninety miles an hour and says it was an accident I want to believe him then too, no matter how sad he looks to be awake the next day. I want to tell Jimmy everything's going to be okay and I want to tell him this for fifteen years while he goes from job to job and leaves town and comes back and when Jimmy straightens up so to speak and joins a church and marries a girl from the church who always smiles I want to tell him I'm proud of him even though his eyes look flat now, like Jimmy's skipped class and he's not coming back. I want my pop to almost not go to their wedding because it's a dry wedding because of the "godforsaken fundamentalist horsecrap" church Jimmy belongs to and I want my mom to ride out the storm like she always does and I want her to cry at their wedding into Pop's hanky and after the ceremony I want Pop to nod a reluctant approval at Jimmy and shake his hand so no one thinks he's gay. I want Pop to dance with Mom at the wedding and I want her to smile at him like she did at their wedding, and I want him to tilt his head just the tiniest bit so she knows he feels the same way but no one else does.

I want to lose my virginity in a car to a troubled boy named Cliff but I want to marry my high school sweetheart Bill. I want the great sadness of my teenage life to be my brief pre-junior-prom breakup with Bill and I want to throw on my slightly ill-fitting white one-shouldered prom dress at the last minute when Bill shows up in a white tuxedo with a white limo and a white corsage and begs forgiveness. I want to maintain a solid B+ average and when I graduate I want to go to typing school to have something to fall back on and I want to work at the local life insurance company where they award me a plaque that says SECRETARY OF THE MONTH three months in a row but even when they raise me 6 percent I want to quit after nine months to be a homemaker. I want Bill to have a dream of moving to Hollywood to be a stunt-man and I want Bill to give up his dream because he loves me, and I want him to buy me a ring from Zales and propose after the lobster buffet on the deck of the casino boat in the next town over. I want to wear a lacy dress with a long train to my wedding and I want my mom to put her pearl earrings on me for something borrowed and choke back tears when she says But you can forget to give them back and I want flower girls and six bridesmaids and I want my wedding photo taken at Sears and I want that photo to be in the paper and I want the word née to be in the copy in front of my maiden name. I want my house to have a cement patio in back and pink impatiens on the front walk and a basketball hoop over the garage. I want Bill to have tools in the garage so he can fix things and I want him to work long hours and put off fixing things and when he comes home late I want to fix him warmed-up meatloaf with extra ketchup, almost burnt, the way he likes it. I want him to make love to me once a month and not try any funny stuff until he tries some funny stuff I really like and then I want him to make love to me twice a month and I want to tell my girl-friends about it. I want Bill to flirt with a woman from out of town who supplies parts for his business and I want him to come close to having an affair but I want him to remember how much he loves me in the lounge at the Marriott and to tell the almost other woman he was about to make a terrible mistake and I want him to cancel her account. I want to suspect this is going on and then I want to tell myself I'm wrong. I want to serve dip and pretzels and Schlitz in cans to my husband, Bill, and his buddies while they watch the Super Bowl and holler at the TV like it can hear them and while I sit on the stoop and smoke my one (stale) cigarette of the week from my gold vinyl cigarette case under the almost-dark five o'clock sky and look at the fast-moving clouds and sitting there I want to think life is good. I want to live where there's nothing to do, where people join bowling leagues and chain-smoke and drink too much and get into fights at bars or get pregnant at the wrong time or by the wrong guy and dream of getting out. I want to read books by V.C. Andrews and I want to watch *Friends* every night at six and laugh and be glad I don't live in New York and I want to subscribe to *People* and I want to want to meet Tom Cruise.

I want to run into my girlfriends at the market and catch up on gossip in the soup aisle and I want to have a girl named Jenny and I want two boys, one named Joe and one named Jason, and I want my girl to skin her knees in the street and I want Joe to play catch with Bill and I want Jason to play with Jenny's Barbies more than Jenny does and I want them all to bring home ribbons for something and I want to see their pictures in the paper with the ribbons and I want them to fight over riding shotgun and who got a bigger piece of pie. I want to use the word *varsity*. I want Jenny and Joe and Jason to be on the varsity anything, and in spite of what Bill says, I want to not assume that my son is gay because he's on varsity cheerleading and I want to say to Bill something like, And anyway what if he is. I want Jenny to have a canopy bed and posters of boy bands and eat one lettuce leaf for dinner and I want her to join a program and gain the weight back and go on a talk show so she can help others and when she's fourteen and meets a cute goth boy I want her to rip her boy-band posters down during a fight with me in which she says that's not who she is anymore even though she kind of obviously is but doesn't want to be because of the goth boy and later I want to find the posters neatly rolled up in the back of the closet and know that I was right. I want Jenny to sneak out at night to meet the goth boy and go almost all the way with him on his black satin cape that he's laid down by the lake but then decide she can't go through with it and after high school I want to send her to school to be a dental hygienist or a real estate agent or a hotel manager. I want Jason to work after school so he can afford Helmut Lang pants and I want Bill to say Helmut who indignantly and when Jason finally comes out to us at sixteen even though it's been pretty obvious since the Barbies I want Bill to almost disown him but later I want to find Bill on the Internet looking up PFLAG on Google and I want him to take photos of Jason pinning a boutonniere on his prom date Todd. I want Joe to wreck his dad's Mustang on the day he gets his license and I want him to be fine but I want him to want something that isn't in our town but not to know what and I want to tell him he doesn't know what because there's nothing to know and that everything good is here. I want him to be the troubled boy that some hopeful girl loves but can't have. I want to send him to rehab twice before he turns seventeen and tell him I'm sorry if I messed him up and I want him to say it was no one's fault and I want him to fill notebooks with his feelings and write stories about big cities and show them to no one and I want a hand-painted sign on Main Street to say BILL & SON. I want Jason to move to New York to become a fashion stylist and commentator on E! and I want Jenny to get engaged to my best friend's son and I want Joe to get his girlfriend pregnant and I want Pop to freak out and say he's not going to the wedding and why can't there be a wedding without shame and I want Mom to talk him down because Joe really does love her and I want Pop to shake Joe's hand at the wedding the way he does and I want to wear a tasteful suit to both weddings and I want Bill to cry at Jenny's wedding and pretend he isn't. I want Mom to die of old age or a heart attack or anything but cancer and I want Pop to die in his sleep a few months later and I want to tell people he died from a broken heart and I want them to nod when I say it and I want to bury Mom and Pop together by the church and put daisies on their graves once a month and tell them about Jason and Jenny and Joe and I want to know without a doubt that they're always with me.

I want to have lots of grandchildren with more J names like Jordan and Jessie and Jeremy and when they come to visit I want to feed them burgers and Tater Tots and whole milk and if they eat macrobiotic at home I want Bill to shake his head and I want to say Well they're in my home now and I want to fill their Christmas stockings with candy canes and trucks and action figures. I want to take care of Bill when he gets sick and before he dies I want to say It was great wasn't it and I want him to say it was and after Bill dies I want to hear that Cliff has overcome his troubles and that he's back in town and I want to start wearing lipstick again in case I run into Cliff and I want to run into Cliff at the market and say, Oh hi Cliff I didn't know you were back in town, and twirl my hair in my fingers like I'm not someone's grandmother and I want to meet him for a soda and listen to his stories of the big city and be glad I never left. I want to start seeing Cliff again and take bus tours of Spain and France with him on senior discounts and call him my gentleman friend and eat croissants with young couples on their honeymoons and tell them stories that begin with Back in the day and I want the kids to wonder if Cliff and I share a room or not and when I get sick I want Cliff to take care of me and say I'm sorry so so sorry for being such a brooding cliché back in the day because I know I really missed out and when I say there's nothing to be sorry for and that it all worked out for the best, I want him to say he's sorry anyway and I want the kids to come and say tender goodbyes before I close my eyes for good. I want my next life to be slow-motiony, with moody skies and grandpas tossing footballs and heirlooms passed down and really good hair and poignant background music. I want it to be like the fifties or the seventies or maybe even the eighties or maybe even some new future decade where things are like they used to be but in a new way. In my next life I want to accept things as they are and when people ask Why I want to say What do you mean why and when everyone comes back for homecoming I want to already be home.

Acknowledgments

Alice Tasman, you just rock, and thanks to everyone at JVNLA as well.

Reagan Arthur, Michael Mezzo, Shannon Byrne, Larry Kirshbaum, Michael Pietsch, Terry Adams, Geoff Shandler, and everyone at Little, Brown, your support and hard work on my behalf still floors me.

Dad, thank you for being my biggest fan.

If you are currently or have ever been related to someone with the name Crane, Corrado, or Zanger, then I love you to bits. Carlsons, Montgomerys, Brandts, Bogens, and Quinns, that goes for you too.

If you live in Kalamazoo, are from Kalamazoo, or have any intention of visiting Kalamazoo in the future, I probably love you, but a special shout-out to Chafe 'cuz he knows why.

Nina Solomon and Bob Leonard, well, you know.

Adam Levin, I haven't forgotten you.

Lisa, Sue, Mary, Anne, Karin (stop with the cakes already!), Caren and TWJob, you are the best booksellers ever and even better friends. Megan, Lott & Joe (of the awesome *Sleepwalk*), you are the cool kids and I just thank you for letting me hang around sometimes. To the good people of the Chicago Public Library, thanks for giving me something shiny! And to everyone at *Stories on Stage*, what a thrill to be included twice. Northwestern, *New City*, the *Reader*, the *2nd Hand*, the *Chicago Tribune*, and the Printer's Row Book Fair, you all make me proud to be a born-again Chicagoan.

Ben, thanks for the happy ending.

✦

About the Author

✦

ELIZABETH CRANE is the author of *When the Messenger Is Hot.* Her work has appeared in numerous publications, including the *Sycamore Review, Washington Square, New York Stories, Book,* the *Florida Review, Nerve,* the *Believer,* and *Eclipse.* She is the recipient of the 21st Century Award from the Chicago Public Library and teaches at Northwestern University. She lives in Chicago.